MW01193351

Tales From Belize
and more

A Collection of Short Stories
Based in Belize and the Cayes

Anna Fuller Lopez Carroll

Tales From Belize

Copyright © Anna Fuller Lopez Carroll

All rights reserved.

No part of this book may be reproduced by any means, nor transmitted, nor translated into a machine language, without the written permission of the publishers.

Condition of Sale
This book is sold subject to the condition that it shall not, by way of trade or otherwise, be lent, re-sold, hired out or otherwise circulated in any form of binding or cover other than that in which it is published and without a similar condition including this condition being imposed on the subsequent purchaser.

Disclaimer
This book is a work of fiction. Names, places, characters, and events are the product of the author's imagination. Any resemblance to actual persons, living or dead, events, or locales is purely coincidental.

Dedicated to John Fuller, my brother,
Anita Carroll-Kos, my daughter, and
Grandchildren, Jonathon and Kira Kos,
and in memory of my brother, George Fuller.

ACKNOWLEGMENTS

*I would like to thank two English teachers from
St. Hilda's College in Belize City, where I attended and
graduated. They were very encouraging to me in my dreams
of writing short stories.*

*Thanks also to my brother John and my daughter
Anita for their support of my efforts.*

*I thank God also for the day I met Nancy Panoch, who has
given me unhesitating encouragement and assistance to
make my dream of over 60 years come true.
I am so excited.*

Contents

Forward

This is mostly a fictional book of stories regarding legends and folk stories in many areas of Belize, formerly known as British Honduras. This country dates back to 1798. Most legends have been handed down through the generations. The names given to some of the areas stimulate the imagination: e.g. Monkey River, Xaibe (a Mayan word pronounced Shy Bay), Crooked Tree, Mauger Caye, Halfmoon Caye, Xanantunich (Mayan for Virgin Rock).

The original settlers were the Mayan Indians, then came the Scottish, the English with their slaves, and the Spaniards, not exactly in that order. Each contributed something—good or bad—to the country's history. Battles were fought; pirates sought shelter; criminals and many political refugees came from neighboring Latin America.

The country boasts of having the second largest coral reef in the world, with innumerable islands or cayes (365 to be exact). It has a varied terrain and climate, ranging from Mediterranean type to semi-desert.

The reefs provide a barrier between the Caribbean Sea and the Atlantic Ocean and are a diver's paradise. In many parts, the land is below sea level. It is swampy in areas, while to the west it is mountainous with vegetation ranging from densely tropical to temperate: e.g. Scotch pines. There are waterfalls and a variety of unusual wild animals. It is also home to the jaguar, iridescent wild turkeys, and others, which are now protected by law.

Customs and Superstitions

The people of Belize are a conglomeration of races and colours from which emerged glorious beauties, as is evident in the many participants of the annual beauty contests held for National celebrations. The people are like masala: hot and spicy.

The basic races are the Mayan Indians, the Caribs, the Ketchi Indians, the original invaders—Scottish, Spaniards, and English with their slaves. Each brought with them unique customs and superstitions. The languages are predominantly English and Spanish, but there are also the dialects of the Mayans, Caribs and the Ketchis, and what is known as "creole", which is a broken form of English mostly spoken by the mixtures.

Some of the customs and superstitions embody things like Negromancy (Obeah, as it is called), teacup and card reading, although progress and technology have almost wiped these things out.

The bush people, i.e. the inhabitants of the densely forested areas, would talk of the "Duende", someone comparable to the Abominable Snowman or Bigfoot. There has been mention of giant alligators and sea monsters, and many stories exist about "Anancy"—an elusive, intelligent spider.

Naturally as the years rolled by and education became widespread, there was more contact with the outside world, and technology became a way of life, so these beliefs were pushed back and practically died out; now they are told as folk tales.

Xanantunich

Xanuntunich! Bewitching as it sounds, it's really a Mayan Indian word meaning "Virgin Rock". It stands 162 feet high on the western border of a veritable paradise in Central America: Belize (formerly known as British Honduras). It has an enchanting, ancient Indian trail leading up to the top. Along this trail, many, many years ago, Desederia lived with her father, mother, and brother in the village of Hatzcap Ceel.

They lived like every Mayan of those times in a hut of white mud bricks, which they made themselves from mud abundant in the area. It had a thatched roof and was one enormous room with one door and two windows. They slept in hammocks. There were no modern conveniences at that time. Water came from the river nearby and Desederia's family had a prosperous plantation that provided all their needs. The only language spoken was the Mayan dialect.

Desederia was the most beautiful girl, with long, black

plaits, flashing black eyes, a smooth olive complexion and a clean, round face that seemed to glow with radiance. Her physique was a perfect specimen of femininity. She walked with her head held high, so that one would imagine she was a Princess.

To her family, Desederia was a valuable pearl, for she could cook, sew, tend the animals and look after the plantation. She was always kind, loving and sympathetic to everyone she came in contact with. She had a voice like a nightingale, and at dusk when the family sat outside and she was sewing, she would sing beautiful Indian songs for them.

Unfortunately there was a dark cloud hanging over her, which made her very sad. She was nearly fourteen years and therefore it was time that she should marry. As was customary, her father had chosen her mate but she did not want to marry him. She had managed to put things off for three moons but last night her father had said, "By next full moon, you will marry Chac Xib."

Chac Xib was a tall, handsome Indian but he had a reputation of being very cruel. Then again, he had the biggest plantation, which meant a lot in that era in parent's choice of suitors for their daughters.

The next day, while Desederia's brother, Teotakan, was working on their plantation, he saw a stranger coming up the trail. He went to meet him, for it was rare that strangers passed that way. The stranger said his name was Kukulcan and that he had come from across the border, from a village called "Plancha de Piedra" in Guatemala. He said he was headed for Xanuntunich.

"Am I on the right trail? I crave inspiration," he said, "for it is now time that I choose a wife, and what better place to go." He smiled. "Perhaps" he continued, "who knows, Mam, the mountain god might answer my prayer and show me my virgin bride."

Teotakan, not being a dreamer, wasn't very encouraging but assured Kukulcan that he was indeed on the right trail and wished him luck.

That evening at mealtime Teotakan forgot to mention the stranger and his quaint way of choosing a wife. It was after supper that Desederia, being very sad, decided to take a walk.

"Maybe", she said to herself, "if I go to Xanuntunich, I might get some inspiration and find a way out of this difficulty." Her feet went pat pat up the winding trail, and she reached the top breathlessly.

She stood with her head held high, drinking in the pure mountain air and felt free and lightheaded. She felt the world seemed a wonderful place to live in, with no cares or worries. She started to pray to Mam, asking him to save her from Chac Xib. As her lips moved in silent prayer, a few yards away stood Kukulcan.

He too had been offering his prayer and as he opened his eyes, he stood enthralled, gazing at Desederia. He thought he saw a vision in answer to his prayer. What a vision!! His heart stood still, yet it seemed... Wait... the vision moved. Silently he said, *this is no vision, it is real.*

With trembling voice, he went forward and said, "Greetings, fair Princess." Desederia was startled, for she thought she was alone. She looked at this handsome stranger and immediately her body seemed to vibrate with a new feeling she could not explain or understand.

"Greetings," she stammered. "Who are you? And what

do you do here?"

"I am Kukulcan and I have come from the west," he replied, at the same time pointing down to Plancha de Piedra, which could be seen at their feet across the border of Guatemala.

"I came here to get inspiration, for I have to choose a wife," he continued. "When I saw you, I thought you were a vision, a vision of my future wife. What is your name?"

"Desederia" she replied. "I too came up here to think. I am to be wed by next full moon, but I don't want to marry Chac Xib, for he is too cruel."

Then she began to sob. Kukulcan put his arms around her to comfort her. Then an idea struck him. "If I can win a battle against Chac Xib, will you be my wife, Desederia?"

She stood on tiptoe and looked him full in the face, then gazed down at her village and at his. Very quietly she said, "Yes, I will."

Kukulcan was happy. He did not know what to say but took her hand in his. "I will win that battle and I will make you the happiest maid in your village" he said. Then he took her in his arms and kissed her. The sun was just going down like a huge red ball, as hand-in-hand they left the top of Xanuntunich. As they walked along, Desederia felt so happy, she softly sang some of her beautiful songs for him.

When they almost reached Desederia's home, who should they see coming towards them but Chac Xib. Desederia was worried and shaking. He had been to see her but she of course was not at home. His face was like a terrible squall when he saw them hand-in-hand.

"Who are you?" he asked Kukulcan. "And what right have you to hold hands with Desederia?"

"Perhaps she likes to hold my hand, and I certainly like to hold hers."

Chac Xib drew his sword and challenged Kukulcan to a battle. "Those are fighting words," he said. "I am betrothed to Desederia and no one but I have a right to hold her hand."

Kukulcan drew his sword and there and then a fight ensued. Desederia was frightened beyond words, for she knew how cruel Chac Xib was, but Kukulcan was a brave man and could apparently defend himself. Chac Xib was breathing very heavily and his hands were bleeding from many cuts. By this time, many of the villagers had gathered. No true Mayan would miss a good fight.

When Chac Xib saw that he was on the losing side, he drew his knife and would have thrown it at Kukulcan with good aim, but Teotakan rushed up behind him and jerked the knife from his hand. On seeing that Kukulcan was definitely the winner, Chac Xib broke through the crowd and fled. There was wild cheering as Kukulcan went to where Desederia stood alongside her parents, shaking.

He said, "Father, by conquest your daughter is mine, but I loved her from the time I saw her earlier on Xanuntunich. I will work hard to make her happy."

The old man smiled and said, "My son, we are proud to have one as brave and handsome as you in our family. Welcome!"

He then announced that Desederia and the stranger, Kukulcan, would be wed at full moon.

The day of the wedding feast dawned with perfect weather. There was more than enough "bolos" and "chich" (typical Mayan food) for all the villagers, and lots to drink. Desederia looked very regal in her white bridal gown done with all the bright embroidered colours of the rainbow. Kukulcan was dressed resplendently like a Mayan god.

The whole village turned out and Kukulcan's family had arrived from across the border. The wedding ceremony began at 6:00 p.m. and was performed by the village's oldest man, as was their custom. There were songs to the gods, then came the "Zapatiero" dance in which old and young participated.

The merry-making continued through the night until the sun came up. Before Kukulcan prepared to settle down in his wife's home—it was customary for the husband to live with his wife's family until his hut and plantation were ready—he said to Desederia, "Let us go to the top of Xanuntunich and carve our names on the rock as a remembrance of our meeting there."

So off they went before the mist surrounding the rock had lifted. More than a hundred years have passed since their names were carved and when one visits the ruins of the Mayan temple built there and sees the hundreds of carved names, the story comes to mind, of when an Indian virgin found happiness on this "Virgin Rock".

Ben Lomond

On entering the Manatee Lagoon from the east, a most fascinating sight meets the eye. Under the lee of a range of bold, majestic looking mountains in the southwest area of Belize (formerly known as British Honduras) in Central America, lies a tiny peninsula that answers to the names of Gales Point.

To the modern tourist, it is a most picturesque piece of God's handiwork; most of its low houses are made of bamboo poles that have been flattened out, bleached, then dried in the sun. The roofs, thatched from the coconut palms, are most attractive on its white, sandy soil.

To add to all this magnetic beauty, the gentle swaying of the abundant coconut palms, coupled with the silvery reflection across the sparkling water of the lagoon, lend a romantic touch to the setting. Truly, it makes a visitor feel that this is indeed God's country where one could spend the rest of his days in lazy luxurious living.

About the year 1870, many Scottish and English families

were migrating to this part of the world, and there were just a sprinkling of houses on the peninsula. These families lived—as the present inhabitants do now—by fishing and cultivating. This took up practically all their time, so that none was left for exploring the beautiful mountain paths that were just across the lagoon to the west.

Now there lived in Gales Point a Scottish lad named Ben Lomond. He was a charming youth with the bluest of eyes that seemed to penetrate one's innermost soul when he looked at you. His hair was the colour of the rising sun and his clean, smooth face, though not handsome, had a charm about it, so that one could not help liking him. He loved the free life he led: fishing, hunting, cultivating and swimming. He was very happy indeed.

In spite of all this serenity, at certain times of the year, when hurricanes are prevalent in this area of the world, the lagoon could be very treacherous. Many strong gales sprang up suddenly, and as quickly as they came, they went, leaving awful disaster in their wake. Hence the name of the peninsula: Gales Point.

One very early morning in such a season, Ben was out sailing in his small boat, doing the day's fishing. He was whistling as the boat glided along, when suddenly a gust of wind filled his sails and almost tipped the boat over. He had his hands full trying to keep the boat steady. Then, almost like lightning, a terrible gale sprang up.

Ben's sails were ripped apart and he had to let the boat take the course of the wind to avoid being capsized. When all was calm again, Ben found himself practically washed up on the western mainland near one of the mountain paths. His boat was ruined; he was hungry and weary, so he decided to try and see if there was any human habitation.

After walking about a mile, he saw coming along the path what he thought was a mirage. He rubbed his eyes and looked again. Still the figure walked on. She was the prettiest girl he had ever seen. She had natural beauty, with golden brown hair that fell in ripples to her waist. This was the crowning glory to a figure that seemed like perfection to him.

Suddenly Ben felt he ought to run away, but he put on a brave appearance, and as she approached him, he said. "Hello, what place is this?"

"It has no name," she said, "but you must be a stranger. I can't recall seeing you in our village."

"Yes," replied Ben, looking into her dreamy brown eyes, "I drifted ashore here after that terrible gale, and my boat is ruined so I can't go home."

"Come with me," she said, "and we shall see what can be done."

As they walked along, she told him her name was Mary and that she had gone to look for a lost pig when the gale sprang up. She had taken shelter in one of the caves nearby.

Ben was curious and she explained, "Just a quarter a mile more along this path are the caves." She told him there was a rough ladder leading down and that at the bottom one could walk in the various rooms. The air inside was very close, she said; so close in fact that only pine torches would give light there. It was also very cold inside, and in the fifth room was a deep cavity down which one could see a subterraneous river whose waters were black and very icy.

As she finished speaking, they reached her village and were met by a very handsome boy who greeted Mary, "My dear, I was so worried about you. Where were you during the gale?"

Just then he noticed Ben and said, "And who is this stranger?"

Ben told him his name and of his experience in the gale and how he met Mary. Bill, for that was the boy's name, was quite interested in Ben and after they had taken Mary home, he offered to help him repair his boat. He invited him to stay with his family. He wanted to know all about Gales Point and what the people did there.

Bill's family treated Ben as one of their own and for many days Ben, Bill and Mary were one happy trio. Needless to say, Bill was very much in love with Mary, but they had not yet decided when they would be married. By this time, Ben was a victim of her charms, though of course she knew nothing of it. He was very careful to keep things to himself.

Now on the day before Ben was to leave to return to Gales Point, Bill took him hunting. They set out at dawn and after trudging for about an hour along the road to the caves, they turned to the right. This new path brought them in another hour to a most beautiful piece of pastureland on the other side of the majestic mountain where the caves were.

As they stood admiring the beauty of the scene and drinking in the pine air, they heard a rumbling noise behind them. Before both of them could get out of the way, a huge mountain cow came charging at them. Bill managed to jump aside, due to Ben's quick shout, but Ben himself was not quick. His foot slipped and he fell to the ground and the mountain cow trampled him. Bill, by this time had his gun out and emptied the bullets into the animal, which tumbled over on its side.

Bill rushed to Ben and found him bleeding and scarcely able to talk. Nevertheless he managed to whisper, "Bill, I am dying. I love Mary though she does not know it. I know you love her too. Marry her as planned and please take care of her like a precious jewel. She loves you too, I know. Make your home here in this enchanting spot and I know you both will find happiness."

Bill tried to make Ben comfortable, replying, "Yes, Ben, anything for you."

"Grant me two favours please?" Ben rasped.

What are they?"

"First, be sure and go to Gales Point and tell my family what has happened to me. Then, second, bury me here that I may be with you and Mary always." He then closed his eyes and breathed his last.

Bill stood still for a minute with bowed head and offered a silent prayer. He was still in a daze from the incident when a shout snapped him out of it. Some villagers were passing and saw his standing figure. He called for help and when they arrived, the scene told its sad tale without words being said.

They helped to bury Ben. Then Bill said, "He was such a brave lad. In saving my life, he gave his own, and he so wanted to live. Let us call this whole mountain and its surroundings after him. Everyone agreed and to this day, there stands "Ben Lomond" a stately mountain and surrounding area.

Many tourists wonder why a Scottish name was given to an almost uninhabited area deep in the jungles of Central America. If mountains could talk or even the offspring of that mountain cow (which the natives call a Tapir)! What a story they would tell!

Mauger Caye

For the whole length of the coast of what is now known as Belize, stretching from north to south, are found some of the most beautiful coral islands in the world. They are known to the inhabitants as cayes (pronounced keys) and to a tourist or casual visitor to this tiny country, a visit to the cayes is a must; otherwise they will have missed the beauty and wonderful feeling of awe that they portray.

These cayes are numerous, being of various sizes and shapes: big ones, little ones, middle-sized ones, long ones, short ones, round ones and oh! so many more. Actually there are 365 of them. Some of them are government owned, some have private ownership, some are uninhabited, while a few are so populated that they have become recognized as villages. They boast a school, church, police station, bank and post office. There are now hotels, bakeries, and even restaurants. With such a menagerie of cayes, one wonders how some came by their varied and odd names.

Hundreds of years ago, long after Columbus discovered that part of the world, there were many people who found their way to these cayes from the mainland of Central America. There was one caye in particular which seemed to attract travelers. Some say it was the magical beauty of the swaying coconut trees in the tropical breeze, coupled with the silvery reflection of the full moon on the rippling waters, but others say it might be because pirate treasure was supposedly buried there. No one really knows.

This particular caye was half a mile in length and less than an eighth of a mile in width at the widest part. It was almost upon the reef. The few settlers, in their primitive way, built their homes out of the coconut palms and thatched the roofs and sides. They spent their time fishing for kingfish, snapper, crawfish, conch and many more. They swam, sailed their boats and dived near the reef to see the wonders that lay beneath the clear blue waters. It was a free life.

One day two boys, Manuel and Raul, went out sailing for fun. Suddenly the wind got stronger and continued to increase. The boys could do nothing; they were so afraid of capsizing and drowning in the raging waters. They tightened their sails and followed the course of the wind. Both were very frightened because they had never experienced such a velocity of wind.

Then the rain began, the thunder clapped and the lighting flashed. In the twinkling of an eye, they were drenched to the skin and the boat began to fill with water. They had an awful time bailing out the water and keeping the boat steady. They could see coconut trees being uprooted and tossed into the sea like blades of grass.

Soon it got dark and still the storm raged. They were cold, tired, hungry and lost by this time, but glad to be alive. Their boat needed repairs, so they prayed to reach land soon. Around midnight the wind abated and they drifted along until day broke. It was so calm and serene, it seemed as if nothing had happened the day before.

They sighted land and, within an hour, they beached their boat and limped ashore. They had reached a fairly large island that is now known as St. George's Caye. They told their tale to the few inhabitants, who were curious about the other cayes. They helped Manuel and Raul to mend their sails and get their boat seaworthy again.

On the third day, they set out with two men from that caye to try and find their own. About 4 p.m. they arrived at what they believed was their caye, but behold! The boys looked and looked and all they could see was a thin strip of land with hardly any vegetation.

"Surely this is not our caye," said Manuel.

"But this is where it should be," replied Raul.

They tied their boat to a submerged piece of coral and waded ashore with their two friends. They stood and gazed around as if in a trance. Suddenly an aged man they knew as Pedro stumbled toward them. His clothes were tattered and torn and he was very bruised. He managed to say, "My boys, thank God you are alive."

He paused and added, "Our beautiful caye is gone. The terrible storm brought the whole sea up and swallowed everyone and everything. I had tied myself to that tree.

That is all that's left. It's like a ghost caye; it's so meager now, like someone lost all his weight. It's also mauger and has given us no pleasure and won't do so ever again."

He sighed and breathed heavily. "I guess we can now name it 'Mauger Caye'." Chuckling crazily, he fainted from exhaustion and hunger. They gave him what assistance they could, but by nightfall, he had passed away peacefully. They buried him under the one solitary coconut tree left standing, which had saved his life.

To this day stands Mauger Caye, which in spite of the strongest storms or hurricanes, though very slim in appearance, can withstand it all. Today, a lighthouse stands on the caye to warn travelers that there are dangerous reefs nearby. This caye is so tiny that on windy days when the sea rises, it is almost submerged in the water.

The Duende

It was the month of May many hundreds of years ago, when only the Mayan civilization existed in Central America. This story took place in the village of Privacion along the western border of Belize in an area known as the Mountain Pine Ridge.

Here the plains rise gradually to the Mayan Mountains and the whole area is covered with Scotch pines and thick jungle growth, interlaced with numerous creeks and streams of fresh, sparkling water. There is even a waterfall called the Bridal Veil.

Being the altitude is so great, the climate is cool and often the colours of the dawn and sunset are mingled with mist. Within this wonderland of breath-taking beauty, legend has it that deep in the forestlands are beings that the natives call Duende. The word means ghost or something seen/unseen. The stories about it are like stories of Bigfoot or Leprechauns in other parts of the world. The natives believe the Duende can bring good or bad luck,

21

and it was rare for anyone to see it.

One evening Amando and his friend, Agustin, who lived in the village of Xavic nearby, were boasting of their hunting powers to the most popular Mayan Indian maid in Privacion. Her name was Ix Can. She had black silken plaits hanging almost to her knees; her olive skin was smooth like velvet, and her black flashing eyes could be as soft and appealing as a deer's. Both the boys were smitten with her beauty, and although she liked them both, in her heart she really loved Agustin. He was tall, erect, had beautiful shiny black hair to match his inky black eyes and his smile seemed to light up his face. Nevertheless, Ix Can said nothing positive to either of the boys.

Amando, on the other hand, was of medium height, slim, with dark brown eyes and curly black hair, and was happy and smiling whenever he was near Ix Can.

As they chatted one day, Amando had a bright idea. He said, "In two days will be the big Fiesta. Why not let us have a contest now?"

"Good idea," said Ix Can. "But what kind will it be?"

"My idea is that Agustin and I will go hunting, and the one who brings back the biggest and most colourful wild turkey will be the winner," replied Amando. He hoped that Ix Can would then make up her mind to marry him, for he was sure he would win.

Agustin said it was a good idea; he silently hoped to win so he could claim Ix Can as his bride.

The boys agreed to leave at dawn and return at sunset as the last shade of red was sinking behind the hills.

Ix Can said, "It is excellent. I will dance with the winner at the Fiesta."

The boys knew this meant she would choose that one as her mate.

In her heart, Ix Can silently hoped it would be Agustin.

The boys went to bed early. At about 4 a.m. they woke and, though it was very cold, they struggled into their clothes, had a hurried breakfast of the customary coffee and tortillas. After twenty minutes they started to wend their way through the thick mist down to the trail.

Within an hour, the sun rose and the mist rolled back like a curtain, revealing the beauty of the countryside in all its splendour Everything was suddenly awake: birds, animals, insects, butterflies. The vegetation was alive and the boys knew this was an ideal day for their quest. They walked for about a mile and a half more, then decided to go off in opposite directions. They arranged to meet in the evening at the same spot to display their spoils before returning to the village.

Amando walked on for half the day before he saw, perched on a very tall pine tree, a majestic-looking wild turkey with shimmering rainbow colours in the sunlight. Its body moved when it preened its feathers.

He thought, *Now here's a noble bird, worthy to take back to Ix Can. I'm sure to win if I can capture it.* Very carefully and stealthily, he moved as close as possible and then steadily took his aim. With a bang, the gun went off and immediately the beautiful bird dropped at his feet. He was overjoyed, for he had never seen one so large and beautiful. With great pains, he mounted it on a large pole so that he could carry it back. Then he sat down near a tree to eat his meal of tortillas and beans. After resting for some time, he started back to meet Agustin. He was confident he was the winner.

Meanwhile, Agustin was not so fortunate. He had walked for hours, eaten his meal of beans and tortillas, and yet all the birds he saw were very small. He was just about to give up hope when he saw a flash of colour in the bushes ahead. He hurried forward and, sitting on a very low tree branch were two of the largest, loveliest wild turkeys. But…sitting with them was a miniature man with a very large hat—so large Augustin could not discern his face clearly. The man was laughing and giggling.

Suddenly Augustin realized he was looking at a Duende. This frightened him; the laugh made him nervous, but he was determined to get one of the birds.

"He's protecting them," Augustin said to himself. Yet he had a positive sense that the Duende would not harm him, because it had not moved. Very softly and stealthily he crept forward, being careful not to step on dried leaves or twigs. When he was near enough to aim, all he could see were the turkeys. As he pulled the trigger, the ground under him gave way and he felt himself falling. He clutched wildly at space, then a strong arm pulled him up near the edge of the hole. He grasped a jutting root and inched his way up to solid ground.

Looking around to thank whoever had saved him, all he could see was the Duende in the distance, laughing and waving goodbye. He waved back, then looked down at the dead bird. It was magnificent. As he mounted it, he tried to collect his scattered thoughts.

He believed that the Duende must have saved him. "It must be a sign from the gods," he said to himself. "I'm sure now that Ix Can will choose me." Nevertheless he decided he would tell no one of his experience; they might laugh at him. Not everyone believed the Duende existed. He was not even sure if *he* did. Maybe he had dreamt it all.

Ix Can did choose Agustin, as his was by far the most beautiful bird anyone had ever seen. Plans were made for their Marriage Fiesta to take place at the next full moon.

"Maybe the Duende will attend," Augustin said to himself. "Of course only I may see him, but I will acknowledge him. He brought me good fortune with the wild turkey and made Ix Can choose me. She is the love of my life."

Ix Can dressed in white and gold with bright colours of red, yellow and green interwoven. She looked like a princess on her wedding day. Agustin was like a handsome Mayan warrior who had captured her. They were very happy together, and after the ceremony, while the celebrations were under way, they took a short walk to make a wish under the full moon, as was customary.

It was then the Duende appeared. He stood far off, laughing and waving. Both saw him and waved back. It was then Agustin told Ix Can of his experience in the bush. Together they decided the Duende must be the love god in disguise.

As they waved together and turned to go back to the wedding feast, the Duende disappeared and they never, ever saw him again.

Caye Glory

Cassiano and Kasmir, two young fishermen who always got a good catch, decided to travel to the southern cayes of Belize to see if they could catch some very large crayfish. They had heard tales of how large they were there.

Crayfish! The word doesn't sound interesting or unusual, but really it is a very delicious food. Once it was not easy to obtain, and people had to pay fabulous amounts for this aquatic rarity. It can be eaten boiled and made into a salad, cooked with rice and even used as a cocktail. Unfortunately this rare delicacy is found only in certain parts of the world. Its natural haunts are chiefly in tropical waters, usually along grassy patches in fairly shallow water and mostly along the reefs and rocks.

Now Belize boasts ownership of the second largest coral reef in the world and has numerous patches of crayfish haunts. A tourist can spend a whole day looking over the side of a fishing boat into mirror-like water and see lots

26

of crayfish on the bed of the sea below. They come in all sizes and seemingly possess almost human emotions and temperaments, the way some of them fight or are elusive if you attempt to catch them.

Around the 1920's there was no crayfish (or lobster as they are sometimes called) industry. It wasn't until Americans from Miami visited the area and made it lucrative that crayfish became popular. Naturally they searched the southern area to catch them, as they were indeed larger there.

Early one Sunday morning Cassiano and Kasmir set sail in their fishing boat, taking with them plenty of crayfish pots, as the snares are called. They arrived quite late at the fishermen's rendezvous, Caye Glory.

The area is very rocky, as the caye is practically on the reef. The water looks almost jade green and is so clear that they could see nearly everything on the white bed patches of the sea below.

Now because the young men were to catch the huge crayfish that lived in this area, they retired early so as to be refreshed at dawn, ready for work. About 4:00 a.m. they arose, had a hurried breakfast of fried fish, bread and coffee, then set sail to go and set their crayfish pots in suitable spots.

They then decided to fish while sailing slowly around the caye on a voyage of discovery. It was not very large and almost uninhabited. The pots had to be left three or four days, but two days later while they were lazily drifting in the area where their pots were set, they gazed over the side of the boat and noted the pots seemed alive with crayfish.

"Oh! Oh!" said Cassiano, "our pots are filled. Let us take them up."

"Yes," replied Kasmir, "but look! It appears as if one pot has a giant crayfish. See how he is kicking up? The pot has turned over."

They threw their anchor overboard and then dove in the water. Very carefully they brought up the pots—one, two, three, four and so on—each with about five or more large crayfish in them. In the last pot, there was such a commotion going on inside. Peering in, they saw one of the largest crayfish they had ever seen. "He sure seems annoyed at being caught," said Kasmir.

With a great deal of trouble they managed to get that pot on board their boat. Then their eyes grew round and large with surprise. He was huge, almost one foot long with eyes like huge beads, and from the way he was kicking up and moving his eyes, he was deadly furious at being imprisoned. The boys thought he must be the King of the Crayfish, if such a thing existed.

With cautions hands, they removed the other crayfish from the pots and put them in crocus sacks.

"Now for the giant," they said together.

They started to open his pot slowly and carefully, but he kicked up such a fuss that Cassiano's hand was soon covered with blood and he had to shout, "Wait. Let us think of the best way to get this monster out."

Kasmir then tried but received a number of cuts and jabs for his trouble. Eventually between them, using a stick called by the natives a "kisskiss", they got him out on the deck. "Now, let's get him in a sack," they said in unison. Both had visions of being interviewed for the newspaper about this catch, but the eyes of the crayfish flashed angrily in the morning sun and before they knew what was happening, the giant slapped Cassiano with his huge tail so hard that Cassiano fell overboard.

Seeing this, Kasmir turned to get a club to kill the crayfish. Before he could reach it, the giant had slipped swiftly overboard into the water. Before their astonished eyes, they saw him rushing along the seabed, probably to his lair. He went at a rate that could have won any gold medal in an Olympic race.

Both fishermen sighed in relief, for to tell the truth, they were glad to be rid of him. Then Kasmir said, "Who will believe our story? They will say we are telling fish tales."

Nevertheless, they decided that they had cuts and bruises to prove it. Yet they vowed that Caye Glory would not see them again, certainly not to catch crayfish.

"Oh, no!" said Cassiano. "Not even if $500.00 was paid for that monster."

"I agree," said Kasmir. "I would not like to tangle with him again. We will content ourselves with fishing in our home waters in the north, where the crayfish are safe to handle."

Beyond the Reef

Jonathon lived with his brother Jamison on an island between Jamaica and the Spanish Main, as the mainland of Central America was then called. This was around the year 1800 when that part of the world was still in its discovery stage.

There was difficulty in travelling, due to the fact that only sailing boats were used, the weather was unpredictable, and piracy on the high seas was almost a profession. Yet adventurous folks loved the thrill of it all.

These two brothers were very wealthy, possessing rolls of beautiful, expensive cloth, handmade laces, gold necklaces, belts, earrings, and unusually designed rings of gold and silver studded with precious stones. All were worth a king's ransom and had been acquired

on trips when they looted unsuspecting vessels passing their area.

These items were handy as gifts to the women they met when they visited the large islands nearby on buying trips, and they also did much feasting and riotous living.

Nevertheless, the brothers were getting worried because things had reached the stage where fellow robbers in the vicinity would think nothing of looting them, burning their house down and even killing them for their treasures. They were well known and had quite a reputation. They began to brood and tried to come up with a solution. They even thought of burying their treasures and making a map to mark the spot, but felt that would be too easy a target.

One day Jonathon said, "Brother, let's leave this island and travel westward, taking our treasure. From the tales we have heard, in that directions there are numberless beautiful, uninhabited islands full of rich vegetation. We can find one, settle down and live peaceably like lords."

Jamison agreed with this idea and immediately they began to make preparations.

The spirit of adventure was upon them and they kept their plans to themselves. Before sunrise on a clear day in April, they set out in their sailboat "Miranda", having spent most of the nights getting their things on board. Their larder was well stocked and their treasures were safe in huge chests. They sailed smoothly along for about four days with ideal weather. They were very happy.

On the fifth day they noted a speck on the horizon. Peering carefully, Jonathon said, "Can it be that we are near an island already, or is that the mainland?"

Just about then, the wind died down and it became

calm. The boat moved very slowly. "Well, better head in that direction," said Jamison. The sea became glassy, the heat intense and becalmed and the calm was eerie. Even the fish in the clear waters appeared expectant. The boys had never before experienced this kind of atmosphere, and the silence was frightening.

Their boat drifted nearer and nearer what they now recognized as a caye, although they were still beyond the reef. This usually lies about a mile or so in front of the cayes. Looking to the east, they saw that the island was large, thickly covered with coconut trees and at one end, large rocks stood like sentinels in the setting sun. The caye seemed to resemble a half-moon crescent. Then and there they decided to call their caye "Half Moon Caye".

By morning a faint breeze stirred. It grew stronger until by midday, it got so strong they had difficulty with the sails. Within an hour, they were in the midst of a terrible storm. The storm whistled past them, and before they could lower the sails, they were ripped to ribbons and the brothers had to concentrate to keep their boat afloat. Waves were like huge mountains and the fury of the water would have washed them overboard, had they not had the quick wit to lash themselves to the mast. The Miranda was tossed like a cork in the raging waters and the boys could barely open their eyes because of the force of the rain and salt spray. Their clothes felt like they were being torn from their skin. They were being taken nearer and nearer the reef and were horrified to think what would happen when the boat hit it. They knew the reef was as sharp as the finest swords, and in a matter of seconds, they or their boat could be torn to shreds and swallowed up in the churning waters.

After about three hours of this horrible punishment, the wind started to lessen in velocity, and by dusk they found themselves in calmer waters within the reef and almost on the beach of the caye.

They loosed themselves and crawled about the boat, only to discover that most of their food was gone, and definitely all their precious jewels and valuables had been washed overboard just beyond the reef. They had seen the chests sliding overboard but could do nothing to save them. They got out and pulled the boat near the beach and secured it to a rock. They got their belongings and food and prepared to make camp for the night.

Among the debris on their boat, Jonathon found a most beautiful shell. He looked at it with a sad heart then passed it to Jamison, saying, "This is all we have to remind us of our wealth and terrible experience."

Jamison admired it then held it to his ear for a moment. Suddenly he exclaimed, "Listen, Jonathon, listen! Listen to the sound of the great waves roaring beyond the reef."

Jonathon took it and listened. "We must treasure this shell, for it is our only reminder when we listen to it, that all our treasures lie 'beyond the reef' of this Half Moon Caye."

Who knows, maybe some fortunate person may find their treasure, but people, that is what happened "beyond the reef" and how that caye came by its name. Today, if you do find a seashell, hold it closely to your ear and you are sure to hear the roar of the sea "beyond the reef."

The Waterspout

This is a factual story. About twelve Girl Guides and I, their leader, were travelling from Belize City to Caye Caulker in a 25-foot sailing sloop for a weekend campout. It was May and the day was beautiful with bright sunshine. The wind was blowing lightly and the boat glided along smoothly.

At about 3:00 pm., as were singing and laughing, we suddenly noticed that the skies were beginning to get dark and that the sun was hiding behind ominous clouds and there descended an eerie calm. We asked the captain if a tropical storm was brewing, but he said no.

Yet he quickly took down the sails and said he would use the outboard engine. Then he ordered me and everyone to sit down in the bottom of the boat. "You kids are only eleven and twelve years old. Please do as I tell you and you will be safe." He continued, "On no account move around or get up. This sudden change in the weather is the herald of a "waterspout". He told us it could be dangerous to a boat of our size, as the spout was going to be quite near.

We asked what a waterspout was because we had never heard of it. "You kids are in for a most spectacular vision, a treat well worth seeing and experiencing. Keep your eyes open and look towards the east for it will all be over in seconds."

We were all very intrigued. We didn't know what to expect, but as we watched, the skies grew darker and darker. Then we noticed the clouds to the far east started to gather together like a bunch of flowers. Instantly we saw that the wind in the east began to blow very furiously, almost in circles, until we could hear it roaring like a freight train in the distance. The bunched clouds began to take the shape of a huge black funnel with the narrow end coming from the sky. As the tip reached the sea, there was a mighty whirring sound, almost as if a huge helicopter was nearby getting ready to take off. The sea around the funnel was foaming and surging and rising up into the funnel, sucking up with it fish and anything in its path. It was an awesome sight; we all simply stared, not talking or moving. Actually we were terrified.

All this went on for a few seconds, though it felt like minutes to us. Then the sounds diminished and the tip of the funnel began to get shorter and shorter until it was enveloped back into the sky.

This whole episode took less than five minutes and was about a quarter of a mile from our boat. The clouds immediately cleared, the sky was blue and the wind blew lightly again. We felt we had seen a mirage or had a dream.

"So that is a waterspout," we all chorused.

The captain said, "Yes, and you are extremely fortunate because, as you know, it is an awesome sight, but it is rare that anyone gets such a first-hand view so near."

I would personally say it is definitely not something made to order and it is unforgettable. It displays the wonders of nature. We were told this is one way the clouds get their water to turn into moisture and rain. It is as vivid now in my mind as it was some sixty years ago. I doubt I will get to see another one.

The Lights That Never Went Out

Hector Jones, a former sailor with a zestful personality was working as lighthouse inspector. Every two weeks his job took him to lighthouses: one in the north and one in the south.

This was in the early 1900's. As one traverses the beautiful rippling blue waters of the Caribbean near the Belizean coastline, one comes upon tiny coral islands, some near the reefs and some almost upon them. Most are uninhabited and the only signs of life might be about half a dozen coconut palm trees, a small house built on stilts and a tall, white lighthouse, whose beacon light is electronically controlled. This light acts as the guiding star to the cargo ships that enter between the reefs to reach the mainland port of Belize.

These reefs are treacherous, their jagged jaws ever waiting to chomp a ship to bits if an error is made and the ship doesn't go through the proper channel, and there are submerged reefs.

Now within a month, two ships had been wrecked on the reefs and Hector was extremely puzzled and worried over these incidents. He realized that it could mean real trouble for him. That morning his employer had called him in and said, rather rudely Hector thought, "Things are becoming embarrassing, Hector. These wrecks have got to stop. The lights must be properly checked or I shall have to find another inspector."

Hector was boiling mad. Mr. Ross seemed to think it was his fault that the wrecks came about. Nevertheless he controlled his temper and calmly replied, "Give me one week to work freelance and I will find the answer or resign my job."

"Well," drawled Mr. Ross, "you'd better solve the problem indeed, or the job will be off."

Walking along the promenade, Hector mused and tried to find a solution. Eventually he decided he would spend a night in each lighthouse. Then he felt he could safely say that the lights were not at fault. True, it meant a long and dreary vigil, but his job was at stake. His wife, Mary had not enjoyed his company for years while he was at sea and now he was not going to give up this land job so easily.

He kept his plan to himself. He fitted out his motorboat and merely told the office clerk the next day that he was going on an extra inspection trip.

The clerk eyed him suspiciously but said nothing, as it was not unusual for an extra tour to be done. He checked the tour into the outgoing book.

As Hector went outside and turned the corner of the street, the clerk picked up the telephone. "Ken here," he whispered, "I have a bit of news. Our friend has gone off on an extra tour."

"Thanks a lot pal," the voice at the other end said, "that means he'll go south tonight eh?"

"Yes," Ken replied, "he always goes south first."

The voice said, "It's lucky we have a ship coming in tonight in the north."

As he put the telephone down, Ken smiled to himself, thinking how easy it was to make $100.00 with just a phone call. "After all it endangers no one's life," he told himself.

Hector had decided to go north first but had mentioned nothing to the clerk. He reached the caye early that evening and beached his boat, making sure it was securely tied up, for the sea was rather choppy and the wind might rise at night. At this stage he certainly wouldn't want to be stranded.

He went into the house and decided to rest in preparation for the long night watch. At 7:00 p.m. the alarm went off. Taking a thermos of coffee and some sandwiches, Hector climbed the high ascent to the lighthouse. Inside the miniature room, all appeared in order. He used his stopwatch to check the revolutions of the light.

"Yes, they are correct for the last ten minutes" he said to

himself. He checked the glass windows and found they were absolutely clean, without cracks. Everything was in tip-top shape.

It wasn't an easy job sitting up all night, watching the light and checking every ten minutes to see whether the timing was correct. His limbs became cramped and as the night wore on, he could hear the waves buffeting themselves on the reef nearby.

Peering through the windows, all he could see was darkness; even the stars seemed reluctant to come out. At about 2:00 a.m., as the wind whistled past the lighthouse, Hector began to feel sleepy. He drank some coffee, remembering his grandmother's saying, "A strong cup of coffee keeps one awake." Hector knew he couldn't afford to fall asleep.

As the wind howled outside, Hector kept a lonely vigil until 5:00 a.m. arrived. He knew the sun would soon be out and the greyness of dawn would peep out. He started his perilous descent so he could return to the house and rest before starting back to the mainland.

As he reached the ground, he looked towards the reef. "No! it can't be," he said. He took out his binoculars and clearly saw that a cargo ship was floundering on the reef and that lifeboats were endeavouring to brace the high seas and cross into calmer waters inside the reef.

Hector was so dazed that all he could do was sit down on a fallen tree stump. He felt weak. How could that ship be wrecked when the lights never once went out last night?

He couldn't understand, unless...but his mind refused to think it....it had been deliberately wrecked.

He wondered. Or maybe the man on watch fell asleep and was too late and unable to steer the ship off the path of the rocks and therefore blamed the lights. The small cargo ship usually had only one man on watch at night. All these ideas ran through his mind, but he decided to keep them to himself.

He pushed off in his motorboat and steered in the direction of the lifeboats. As he got near, he shouted and asked if they needed help.

Scanning the faces, he could see their surprise. They told him that the lights were out: hence this shipwreck. They said they were fortunate to get away with their lives.

Hector asked how it was they couldn't see the light. One surly looking man said, "I was on duty and saw no light or else I would have known where to steer, wouldn't I?"

"That's funny," said Hector, "the lights were on all the time. I was in the lighthouse keeping watch all night"

"In the lighthouse?" queried the man.

"Yes," said Hector, "I was there to see that the lights never went out."

"Ha!" the man said," then you had better check the machinery because the lights definitely went out. You know this wreck will cost the insurance company a tidy sum."

"I guess so" Hector agreed. Keeping his thoughts to himself, he towed them back to port, then he went off to the shipping office to make his report.

Mr. Ross was livid with rage when Hector told him that another wreck had taken place. "You are fired," he shouted. "I thought you were going to solve the problem."

Very quietly and calmly, Hector said, "But I have."

Mr. Ross stood still. "How?"

"Let us go to your office where it is private," Hector said. There he related how he had spent the night and the light never once went out.

"Then they deliberately wrecked the boat," said Mr. Ross. "But how are we going to prove it? It is their word against yours and you were in the lighthouse. It won't stand up in court."

Hector suggested that they get in touch with the insurance company and arrange a time when another ship was due to come in. Mr. Ross promised to do this and said he and Hector would talk the next day when some arrangements would be made.

As soon as Hector passed the outer office, the clerk said, "I see you gave false information. You did not go on the usual tour."

Hector replied, "I have the boss's sanction to do as I like."

"Oh, boss's pet, eh?" snarled the clerk. This confirmed Hector's suspicious that the clerk was working with the men and giving information out about which lighthouse he would be visiting. He decided that the clerk needed watching.

As Hector walked home, he was aware of being watched. On arrival, his wife told him that someone had come to ask when he would be home. Now Hector knew he was right in his deductions, so he decided not to go out again, but to get to bed early and catch up on his sleep.

At about11:00 p.m. the phone rang. Sleepily he answered it. "Hello, Jones here."

A muffled voice said, "Ross speaking. Can you come to my house right away. I have something important to talk over with you."

The voice sounded odd but Hector said, "O.K. I will be right over." Grumbling to himself because his sleep was disturbed, he dressed quickly and, on second thought, put his revolver in his pocket. He told Mary he would not be out long.

The night was dark and he walked along warily, always on the alert. As he was about to turn into South Street, he glimpsed a shadow. Had he not been quick enough to throw himself into the bushes nearby, he surely would have received a fatal blow. The shadow ran off, but not before Hector fired, and from the cry he heard, the person must have been hit.

On reaching Mr. Ross's house, he found it in darkness and realized he had been called out on a ruse. All this confirmed his suspicions, but how to prove it? These people appeared ruthless. He was now worried about Mary too.

The next morning, he told Mary a bit of the problem and asked if she would go and stay with her sister for a few days. Until things got settled.

When Hector reached the office and told Mr. Ross of the incident, he was informed, "I have spoken to the insurance company and they are holding up payment, pending an investigation."

Hector then outlined a plan he had. With the cooperation of the police and the insurance company, they would get their proof. Hector would put his plan into action.

Later on he went into the local bar and, in conversation, announced confidently to the bar-keeper—who he knew to be the local gossip—that he had discovered accidentally that the wrecks were deliberately done to collect insurance. When asked what he intended to do about it, he coolly replied, "Oh, tell the police I guess, unless... Just then someone came up and he was unable to finish.

The policeman assigned to stay in the bedroom with Hector was a pleasant chap, calm and assured, which helped Hector's fraying nerves. Suddenly there was the faintest sound. Tensely they listened, but it was only the wind blowing a weakened branch of the flaming tree near the window. The wait was strenuous. Hector looked at the bed, made up to look like he was asleep in it.

Just then, he sensed that someone was in the room. The hair on the back of his neck tingled. The figure moved toward the bed, striking it with a vengeance. In a flash, the policeman darted to the figure and a scuffle ensued. Hector switched on the light. It was the same surly looking man who spoke to Hector the morning of the wreck.

He spat out, "You infidel, you and your smart ideas!"

"That's enough," said the police, cuffing him as the insurance agent and Mr. Ross came on the scene.

A week later as Hector came down the Court House steps, he was congratulated by all and sundry for solving the problem of the wrecks. He was told that some of the local people had begun to think there was something ghostly connected with the wrecks. Hector's reply to it all was, "My inspiration was Mary. She has depended on me so much since I got this inspector's job, and we are enjoying being able to be together. I had to do something drastic to keep my job. I am glad it is all over now and that lights never went out."

Maid of the Jungle

Alighting from the plane at Rio Grande Airstrip in a remote town of Belize in Central America, twenty-five year old Jack Hall's greenish eyes opened wide. He looked around with admiration at the wide expanse of tropical growth stretching before him. He wiped the sweat trickling down his flushed face and pushed back his brown, limp hair from his forehead.

Already Jack was beginning to feel the heat and humidity. The place had not looked much like virgin land from the window of the plane, but now he thought the prospects looked good for him to obtain the desired wood he was seeking.

An older passenger walking alongside him commented, "Beautiful land, isn't it? A pity the natives these days are so afraid to work in the jungle eh?"

"Afraid?" enquired Jack curiously, getting worried and yet intrigued. "Why should they be?"

"Oh! Some silly thing about a Maid in the jungle, as far as I could gather on my last trip," his companion said.

"Well, I have come to get a shipment of Ziricote wood and I am jolly well going to get it, Maid or no Maid. No jungle superstition is going to deter me," Jack replied in a positive tone.

"I like your spirit, my boy, Good luck! You will surely need it." So saying, the man strutted off to the Immigration office.

Later on that day, as Jack sat down to lunch at his hotel, he recalled the conversation he had in Miami with George Bent, his Manager. Jack was the supervisor in the Florida Wood Company where they worked. Bent had told him, "Fail to obtain that Ziricote and we'll all be out of a job. I am depending on you, Jack."

Jack felt he could not let George down. His handsome face took on a determined look as he clenched his fists, saying silently, "I must succeed. I simply must."

As he sipped a cool orange drink, he saw his newly acquired native friend, Armando Ruiz, sauntering up the street. Armando was very carefree and friendly and had taken an immediate liking to Jack when they met at the airstrip.

Armando came up and shook hands with Jack, saying, "No luck my friend. The workers absolutely refuse to go into the jungle. Seems you'll have to take the next plane back. I'm so sorry."

Jack pulled out a chair and said, "Sit down Armando."

Armando looked startled and serious.

"First of all," Jack said, "please understand this. I am NOT going back without that Ziricote. The next thing is we have to think of a way to get the wood and forget about this Maid of the Jungle thing. It is just silly superstition."

"Right", agreed Armando, "but my countrymen thrive on superstition, and it's hard for them to overcome it."

Jack took out his billfold and showed Armando a wad of money. The U.S. currency meant a lot to a native, for their existence depended mostly on what work they could do for the U.S. Companies. Native payrolls were not much.

Armando looked impressed and asked, "Well, how much of a bonus are you prepared to pay?"

"Double your usual pay if we can get the wood out within the week," Jack replied. Silently he added, *if nothing else attracts them, that will.*

Armando's brown eyes danced mischievously and his round, suntanned face took on a thoughtful look. He leaned back in his chair and closed his eyes. Jack was silent, waiting.

Suddenly Armando jumped up, saying, "I've got it."

"Got what?" asked Jack, bewildered.

"Listen carefully," said Armando. "My family is very large you know: brothers, uncles, cousins by the dozen. What I will do is to organize them to do the job. We will say we are going on an excursion into the jungle. We will cut the wood and at the same time enjoy ourselves. If the Maid of the Jungle chases us, well, we'll run and you can't say we didn't try. If we don't see her, then we will be richer than when we went in, eh? And you will get you wood. O.K.?"

Maid of the Jungle

"Excellent idea, Armando," said Jack. They stood up and shook hands on the deal.

As they parted, Armando slapped his chest and said, "Don't worry, my relatives dare not refuse the great Armando anything." Whistling a tune, he winked and sauntered off.

It was all arranged the next day. Early in the morning Jack, Armando and a group consisting of about twelve of Armando's relatives started their "excursion" into the jungle. This was why they hid their saws, machetes, etc., but took along lots of food and their guitars.

As Jack watched them, he had qualms and wondered if they would really work or just have a pleasure trip. He sighed and trotted alongside Armando.

After travelling some miles deep into the jungle, they found a very suitable site not far from a native village, according to Armando's geography. They pitched camp. That night there was merry-making, singing with their guitars, doing native dances and telling jokes in their native language, and some in English for Jack's benefit. No one seemed to have any fears at all, and Jack began to feel content.

At the crack of dawn, Armando roused everyone. Jack marveled at his leadership. He made them clear the banging creepers and pinpointed the best Ziricote. He worked them diligently until evening when he said they could relax. Laughingly he told Jack, "Remember this is an excursion."

After two days of hard work, Jack felt very confident that all would be well. As he could do very little in the camp, he decided to go hunting to try and secure two

49

beautiful wild turkeys he had seen hovering in the area the day before.

Everyone was loud in warning Jack about the Maid of the Jungle, but he told them, "I will bring her back too, then no one will have to worry about coming to the jungle again to work."

After walking some distance Jack glimpsed two wild turkeys that he imagined were the same ones he previously saw. He began stalking them. They were beautiful with feathers in an array of iridescent colours that shimmered in the sunlight. He was sure Armando would be elated if he presented him with these stuffed turkeys as a memento.

The birds alighted after a time on a rather low hanging branch. Jack moved stealthily to get close enough for a good shot. He trod very carefully, getting nearer and nearer, when suddenly the ground beneath him gave away and he plunged down into a deep cavity. He was so shocked he didn't even shout for help. He managed to cling to a stump while failing, and there he hung, trying to find a foothold. Slowly and painfully he pulled himself up on to a tiny ledge in the darkness.

He discovered that his leg was injured as he crouched down. He started shouting for help in the hope that a passing native might hear. After a while, he felt hoarse and then found he could barely see the sun's rays so it must be sinking in the west.

He realized he was stuck until morning when Armando was sure to organize a search party. Overcome with tiredness he propped himself up and immediately fell asleep. Suddenly he was awakened by a very brilliant light that almost blinded him. Blinking his eyes, he saw looking down at him a most beautiful girl in a shimmering white gown with a tinseled headpiece over long, black, silken hair. Her smile and shiny black eyes were warm and comforting as she dropped a thick silver cord down to him and beckoned to him to climb out.

Although startled, he trustingly took the cord and started the precarious and painful ascent. She assisted him and, after much difficulty, he reached the top where she held him with strong arms and led him limping to a nearby tree so he could prop himself up against it. He sighed with exhaustion as she handed him a cool draught out of a tiny cup. He drank thirstily, then turned to express his gratitude.

Lo and behold! The girl was nowhere in sight. She seemed to have vanished into thin air. Try as he might, he could not keep his eyes open and fell asleep.

Awakening, Jack opened his eyes slowly, then very wide as he stared at the vision caressing his forehead. "How do you feel?" she asked him.

He tried to get up but discovered his right leg hurt too much. "I feel pretty bad I guess," he said laughingly, "though you seem to be taking pretty good care of me."

Before she could reply, there was a shout of, "Hello there," and Armando arrived with a search party. "Ah-ha!" he said with a twinkle in his eye. "Jack, you appear to be enjoying yourself in Agida's good hands. We were worried sick over you, thinking the Maid of the Jungle had captured you."

"But she has," retorted Jack, "and here she is."

"Oh, no." sighed Armando, laughing. "Don't tell me your brain is affected." Sweepingly he introduced Agida as being from the nearby village. Jack was puzzled. Then he noticed the cup still held tightly in his palm.

"Examine this," he said. "The Maid of the Jungle gave it to me."

Everyone eagerly came forward to see it and discovered it was pure silver with exquisite workmanship and markings. In chorus they cried, "The Maid of the Jungle must have rescued you before Agida found you. This proves the Maid is not to feared but loved, because her work is good." Everyone was overjoyed.

Jack realized his troubles with getting the wood cut and shipped were over. Nevertheless, he was still puzzled over the incident but decided to keep his own counsel. He had fallen for the charms of Agida, who in his heart was the Maid of the Jungle. He asked himself, "If she isn't, who then got me out of the hole and gave me this cup. Maybe I dreamt it all." It was indeed very confusing, though fascinating.

Turning to the crowd, he said, while winking at Agida, who blushed prettily, "I told you I would bring back the Maid. Agida will always be *my* Maid of the Jungle. I would like to take her back with me to Florida and let her continue looking after me there."

"Oh, she will, she will." They all said. Agida turned a deep pink as Jack held her hands and squeezed them reassuringly. He might not ever know the truth about what really happened, but he knew he was enthralled with Agida and halfway in love, and she was no superstitious vision. He was not going to argue over the cup either. He knew that was real.

Hurricane Abby in Belize

It was about 10:00 a.m. while I sat pounding my type-writer in the Police Department where I work, when someone came up to me and said, "The cocktail party this evening has been cancelled."

"Cancelled?" I asked. "Why?"

"There's a hurricane warning out, that's why," the Policeman told me.

I was astonished, for to tell the truth, as I looked outside the window, the weather appeared absolutely perfect to me. The cocktail party had been arranged by the Police Department to bid farewell to the Colonial Secretary. He was leaving the country in four days time to transfer to Mauritius. I thought to myself, *well if the Weather Bureau says there's a hurricane out, there must be one.*

On the midday news, the local radio station reported

news about Hurricane Abby. It certainly was in the vicinity of British Honduras, as Belize was then called. Abby, the news said, was in the Bay of Honduras, to be exact. It did not sound very powerful to me; the highest winds were estimated at 70 miles per hour. I dismissed the whole thing from my mind rather quickly.

When I returned to work that afternoon, I was struck by the preparations being carried out at Police Headquarters. The main office, the canteen, etc. were being cleared in readiness for use as Public Safety Shelters, just in case Abby did strike the country. At 4:00 p.m., when I left for home, I could sense that the whole town was agog with excitement, stemming from fear of the hurricane. The first warning red flag had also been hoisted in the main square. By this time, the weather had suddenly changed to occasional showers with light winds and extreme heat in the interim. As I drove home, I could hear sounds of hammering where windows and doors were being barred up and there were even men perched on ladders actually doing their nailing up on the outside.

Abby was certainly going to have a tough time doing much damage I thought. The streets were busy with people hurrying along, all preparing for the onslaught. I met friends who told me, "Aren't you frightened? I am going to El Cayo, in the west, where it is mountainous and not so dangerous."

I replied, "I'm not scared, after all there is a saying: "Unless God keeps the city, the watchman wakes in vain."

My friend said, "My dear, I'm taking no chances. I would rather not be in the city at all."

Another friend said to me, "You appear as if you don't believe there's a hurricane headed this way."

I said, "Sure I believe, but the news didn't say it would hit Belize, and in any case at the rate it is travelling, it couldn't possibly reach here before midday tomorrow."

She said, "Hm!! you'd better bar up your home or you might be sorry."

I laughed and said, "One thing, I'm sure of is that I shall say my prayers extra well tonight."

On and on through the evening until late at night, people either left town for El Cayo or barred their windows and doors.

Later on I even saw people who seemed to be removing items from their homes to places they thought more secure.

All through the night, the hammering went on; the radio station kept broadcasting the latest weather bulletin hourly so that the population could know what the situation was. People were moving about excitedly.

Around 9:00 p.m. it became definite that Abby would hit the southern part of Belize, i.e. Stann Creek and the Toledo Districts. The people there were advised to take precautions for the protection of life and property. From early in the evening, all boats in the whole area up to the Yucatan peninsula were advised to either stay put in their ports or move in towards the river where it was calmer and safer. The boats in Belize Harbour all went up the Belize River so that the shoreline looked bare.

Had Abby struck Belize, I am sure there would not have been much damage done and I am sure no lives would have been lost; the highest winds reached 100 miles per hour. The population of Belize could have won any Boy or Girl Scout test of "Be prepared", for indeed they were ready and well prepared for Abby. No one can blame them for their preparations, for when Hurricane Janet struck the northern districts in September 1955, those who were not ready certainly paid the penalty (some with their lives) for their unpreparedness. The local doctor in 1955 said when interviewed on the radio, "It was a day I shall never forget as long as I live."

Thus, I think every hurricane warning brings fear to those who have never experienced a hurricane, and a fearful memory to those who have passed through one.

Caye Caulker

Life on an island located amidst the coral reefs of the blue Caribbean is mostly very carefree and tends to let one feel lazy and forgetful of time itself. Yet to a visitor studying the situation deeply, vital facts seep out. I will try to tell you a story about one such island I visited.

Actually it is called a caye (pronounced key) and I was fortunate to visit it in the month of May many years ago in the early 40's. The people were mainly of Spanish descent; they were half Latins and half creoles, most of them fishermen by trade. Most are short, of erect gait. Vibrant personalities, most of them: friendly, warm-hearted and carefree, though hard-working. Their skins were smooth, bronzed different shades by the kiss of the tropical sun; their hair was always neatly combed. All in all they looked a pretty healthy lot.

As I walked around the caye, I was certain of a welcoming smile or nod as I passed their homes. The women were mostly occupied with house duties, but never too busy to stop and greet a stranger or newcomer and always asked if he or she was enjoying the visit to the caye.

Saturday night seemed to be the festive night when a dance was put on, held in the open square near the single Police Station. I was told these dances were held mostly in the months of April, May and June but could extend to August. Although it seemed just another happy occasion, there was much to learn. Everyone seemed happy; the majority spoke Spanish, and some English and Spanish. And their attire! What a variety: crinolines, blue jeans, leather shoes, running shoes, and quite a majority in bare feet.

Then came Sunday morning when church bells rang (there were two churches) and one could see the village folk winding their way there. Afterwards began a real day of rest. The men sat outside their homes in groups, talking about practically everything under the sun. Snippets of conversation I heard were what a man likes in his home; he likes to know his wife has all conveniences, no matter how simple. He likes to know his children will have opportunities in life for education, for travel and to enjoy their childhoods. They discussed international affairs, local politics, all while enjoying the lovely sea breezes that fanned the tall coconut palms.

The women too had their discussions with one another or with a visitor like me. I learned that their hopes and dreams were no different from their counterparts in a big city. Also crime seemed to be at an extremely low level.

One shining fact stood out, and that was that they never grumbled or showed signs of dissatisfaction with their lots in life. They were content and happy with what they had, yet always working to advance themselves. They were relaxed. Perhaps that is why their faces did not betray their ages. They had warmth and affection, which I had not met before, and it is to be hoped that never changes.

The Jade Skull

Deep in the jungles of Central America in the early 1900's there existed a Mayan village named Lubaantum. This was in the country of Belize (then known as British Honduras). Around 1923 or earlier Lubaantum was just another lost or buried Mayan village. It was in excavating that the lost god of the Mayan was found. They believed this god to have power over life and death. He was an exquisite and valuable god in an anatomically correct human skull in every detail, weighing 11 pounds 7 ounces. and made of the most beautiful jade. Even the lower jaw was a separate piece to which the Mayan priests of old would attach threads that allowed them to work the jaw to make it appear that it could talk, while in their darkened temple.

Faith is the Answer

Robert was the Collector of Customs in the small Central American seaport where I lived with my family. He and his family were next-door neighbors.

Robert was unforgettable, not because of his handsome face, steel grey eyes and slightly wavy brown hair. He was also 6 ft. 1 in. tall and had a very athletic looking body. The fact is, he had a very strong impact on my life. I admired his strength of mind, his jovial personality in the face of insurmountable odds, and how he handled his life. I was amazed at the faith he exhibited.

He was forced into early retirement at age 50 due to a diagnosis of cancer of the jaw, after which he travelled to New Orleans, U.S.A. for surgery, where the doctors removed his jawbones. That was the procedure for that era. Robert returned home on a beautiful sunny day.

Faith is the Answer

Many friends and relatives had gathered at his home to welcome him back. On alighting from the taxi, his first comment to the crowd was, "I'm stuck with this face, so let's get used to it," and he laughed as he touched his jaw.

I was only sixteen years old at the time. I stood affixed, staring at his face, then I immediately ran over to my house and burst into uncontrollable tears.

My mother followed me and tried to comfort me, saying, "You'll get used to it; at least he is alive and seems happy."

I told her, "That's no consolation. I'm not in his shoes and I feel depressed and despondent. Surely he is too?"

His once handsome face looked so grotesque to me. I had gotten a traumatic shock when I saw it. I don't really know what I had expected. For days afterwards I watched from my window whenever he did gardening in his yard and tried to get used to the face. It was a hard task. I kept wondering how his wife and two children didn't seem to be affected, when I was devastated and I wasn't even a relative.

Yet his new face seemed not to be a problem for him. He had such a good grip on himself. He told my father one day soon afterwards, "John, God is good. I thank Him every day for being alive. Who cares about looks? I'm just happy to be alive." Obviously he was a man of faith.

A couple of weeks later, I heard my father say to mother, "Robert is going to grow a mustache and beard. He thinks then his new face won't shock people."

My mother replied, "I think it would at least be more tolerable." The year was 1941.

I must say that indeed the bearded face was more tolerable to me. It hid the physical disfigurement. I was now able to chat with him without getting emotionally up-set. He had known that some people avoided conversing with him because of the impact his face had had when he first arrived back home.

The doctors had forbidden Robert to have alcoholic drinks and he was told not to absorb too much sunlight, both of which he loved. He said, "God will look after me I know, so I will do things in moderation." He was never a regular churchgoer, but now he and his wife attended church every Sunday.

Robert told all his friends and acquaintances, "I will have a drink when I want and I'll use a wide brimmed hat when I go fishing." This was his cherished hobby and he thought he might as well die if he couldn't go fishing. Often he would say, "I know my time here with you all is limited so I may as well do what I enjoy and die happy. God knows what's best anyhow. It's all in His hands."

He entertained a lot, as usual, although his personal food he prepared in an Osterizor. The doctor had given him six years more of life at his last check-up, but he actually lived sixteen years more. Even his wife and brother died before he did.

I think he is an example of what faith will do and what attitude and acceptance of a serious problem does to assist one in coping with life's tribulations. I know I learned a lot about faith from his attitude. Knowing him taught me how to face life with strength, fortitude and to accept things when life deals a bad blow over which we have no control. It teaches us that one should feel good about oneself, put on a happy face, for it prolongs life and makes those around us happy. He certainly enriched my life. As life progressed for me, I have found that whenever I have problems that seem insurmountable, I think about Robert and realize that my problems are minor compared to what he went through. He was a survivor who never lost his faith in God. I then feel that I too can conquer my problems. At age sixteen, one is very impressionable and I certainly have a lasting imprint of Robert's stamina and faith, which has stood me in good stead until now.

Life After Death

I am sure there is life after death. Though my experience occurred some 45 years ago, it is still very vivid to me. I had just passed my thirteenth birthday when I fell sick with high fever. My parents were naturally very concerned and called the doctor, who gave me a needle. My temperature dropped almost immediately but for a couple of days after I suffered weak spells even when sleeping.

One day as I slept, my grandmother, who had been keeping constant watch over me, noticed how deeply I seemed to be breathing and that all the veins about my forehead seemed to be bulging. She quickly saturated a cloth with cologne and gently mopped my forehead until my breathing became natural and I appeared peaceful. Then suddenly I woke up and asked, "Where am I?"

Life After Death

The truth is that I had felt so very peaceful and happy while asleep. I dreamt I was in a canoe travelling along a stream (which seemed like the street in my town that leads to the cemetery). My garment—like all of the people's on the shores and in the canoe—was a long white, shimmering gown, beautiful. Everyone had such an indescribably happy expression on their faces, and I was elated to be one of them. The water was crystal clear, the grass luxuriant and vividly green; the whole atmosphere was one of extreme delightful happiness and contentment. I felt as if I was floating and never wanted to stop. It was ecstasy and I loved it all. Then the canoe stopped at a small bridge—the only one along that street—and I was told to get out, as there was something wrong. As soon as I got out, the canoe moved on quickly and the occupants shouted, "We'll be back another time for you." I was so disappointed I wanted to cry. That was when I woke up.

When my grandmother told the doctor about my heavy breathing and bulging veins while asleep, he said "She probably was on the road to dying peacefully in her sleep, but your prompt action somehow revived her. Be grateful."

Learning About Evil

One particular incident I recall happened when I was sixteen-years-old. I was a Girl Guide selected to represent my country to attend an International Girl Scout Camp being held in East Otis, Massachusetts, USA. I was thrilled and excited but worried, because I was sure my father and mother would not allow me to travel that far alone. The Governor's wife, who was President of the Girl Guide Association, came to our home and talked to my parents and convinced them I should be allowed to go. So I was elected, but then there was the medical test to pass. I was always in good health. When I went to the hospital for my physical, all went well, except the nurse said my temperature was quite high and I probably had a fever—maybe malaria. I knew this could not be true and asked for a re-test; again she said it was high, but I managed to take the thermometer from her unexpectedly and read it myself and it was normal. She tried to stop me but I rushed outside to the doctor and showed it to him. He then took my temperature himself and said it was definitely okay. I later found out that this nurse's niece was the runner-up for the position of delegate and her aunt was hoping to disqualify me. This was my first experience of coming up against evil, and it made me aware ever since not to be naïve and adults are not always to be trusted. Trust has to be earned.

The Beach

The day was bright and cloudless, the sun shone like a golden light, its rays enveloping everything everywhere. Xana sat on the beach hugging her knees closely. Her usual sparkling brown eyes seemed dull and insipid as she tried to focus them on the quivering black dot some miles out to sea in the softly undulating expanse of water.

Her thoughts kept revolving around one question: *Why can't I get Luca to notice me and be interested in me?* Closing her eyes, she indulged herself as she visualized his tall, lean body, broad shoulders and smooth skin, so evenly bronzed by the brilliant tropical sun.

"I wish his shiny black eyes would look at me with desire," she thought dreamily, as she gazed out to sea. The black dot was getting larger as it bobbed nearer and nearer to the shoreline. It was then that Xana noticed that the dot was actually a small boat. She could discern Luca in it, but she noted he was not alone.

The Beach

As the boat reached the beach, Xana saw Caya—the vivacious redhead who had arrived the night before with her family—get out at the other end of the beach. Actually "arrived last night" was not an apt description. Caya had more or less floated into the hotel lobby. Her short-short pink shorts and matching halter-top fitted like an extra skin, revealing her full breasts. Red curls hung in ringlets like a cap around her perfectly etched face. Her eyes had sparkled like black diamonds and her tiny red lips were reminiscent of a delicate rose. As she sauntered past Xana in the lobby with her parents, she smiled and waved her tiny, well manicured hands and said, "Hi, everyone." It was no wonder that Luca had been smitten on the spot with her beauty.

Xana sighed as she watched the scene. Caya leaned over and hugged Luca as she moved off. Her voice floated on the wind as she said, "See you tonight."

Luca pulled the boat onto the beach and as he turned to go, he saw Xana and walked over to where she was.

"Hi," he said, "how are you today?"

"Fine" she replied offhandedly.

"Say, would you care to come with me and my mom tonight to see the dance competition?"

Xana was so flabbergasted at the invitation that she stammered as she replied, "Oh, oh, sure. Won't your mother mind?"

"She'd be delighted to meet you," he said. "I mentioned having met you. I'll pick you up at 6 p.m. Do you think your mom will mind?"

"No, I am sure she won't."

Xana wondered what Caya would think, but decided

not to worry. That evening when Luca picked her up, he seemed delighted to meet her mom and said he would bring her back by 11:00 p.m.

As they were leaving the lobby, Caya was coming in. She looked icily at Xana, and ignored her as she said to Luca, "Will you be back to pick me up?"

Luca replied, "No, I am taking my girlfriend to see the dance competition with my mom."

Caya replied, "Well, well, I didn't think you preferred dead fish when you could have a live one."

Luca was furious and told her, "Get lost kid and grow up. This is the real world, where people are liked for their kindness and inner beauty, not for painted beauty and what you call liveliness. You should learn to dress attractively, be pleasant and thoughtful, then maybe someone will like you for yourself.

Caya burst into tears and flounced off, saying, "You two will be sorry you ever insulted me."

Luca took Xana's hand and said, "Don't worry over her, she will wake up one day and realize her shortcomings."

The Heart of Jade

It was a small, quiet wedding.

"A long and happy life to you both, my dears," Mrs. Grimshaw told Vic and Jenny as she bade them goodbye.

Someone called out that the car had arrived, and as they ran to it, Mrs. Grimshaw commented to her friend June, "Doesn't that unusual pendant Jenny is wearing match her eyes?"

"Yes," replied Vic's father, who was standing nearby, "that's why I chose it for her. It was one of the best antiques I ever acquired. It's called the Heart of Jade. It was one of my wedding gifts to Jenny."

Jorge, one of the caterers, overheard this conversation. Immediately he slipped outside and phoned his brother. "Marco," he said, "tell Jaime immediately that I think I have located the Heart of Jade. A newlywed, Jenny Jones, is wearing it, leaving for Mexico City on her honeymoon."

Jorge was delighted that he had taken the job for the Jones wedding. His suspicions were now confirmed that Vic's father, an antique collector, had indeed bought the Heart of Jade.

While Vic and Jenny were winging their way to Mexico City, supper was being served. Vic noticed a short, swarthy man in a bright blue shirt was sitting across the aisle from them, staring at Jenny's pendant. He whispered to his wife, "That man seems interested in your necklace. Perhaps you shouldn't wear it all the time."

"Why not?" She asked, laughing. "People stare at it because it has an unusual setting. I've never had a real antique before, and I'm fascinated by it. Your dad said it originated in Mexico. Maybe we'll learn something about its history while we're there."

"I suppose you think there's some romance attached to it," Vic said, teasing her.

"Well, there just might be," she retorted, "or who knows? I might be offered a fabulous sum of money for it."

The blue-shirted man whispered to his friend sitting next to him, "Did you hear that, Joe? A real antique is right up our alley. We could probably get fifty grand for it, and who knows what story might go along with it? We might even get more. It surely looks fascinating."

His friend replied, "We have to move carefully, though, Tom."

"I know," Tom answered, "but this is real luck. Here we are on our vacation, and this falls right into our laps. We can't resist it."

Upon arrival at the airport, Vic gave the taxi driver their address, while the two men stood in the shadows and listened. Vic had arranged to stay at a small boarding house, where they hoped to experience a homey atmosphere by staying with a native family.

At breakfast the next morning, Jenny's plain peach-coloured dress was enhanced by her pendant.

As they sat down, Isabelita shouted, "Mama! Mama, *mira*! Jenny has *bonito pendiente*.

Senora Pasos' face looked stony as she turned to her husband, who asked Jenny very solemnly, "Where did you get it, my dear?"

Vic and Jenny looked at each other, puzzled by their hosts' attitude.

Vic told them, "My father gave the pendant to her. It's a genuine antique."

Speaking slowly in English so they would understand him, Senor Pasos said, "I am sure it is, but don't wear it outside your dress. It is not advisable."

Then Mr. and Mrs. Pasos conversed rapidly in Spanish, and though Jenny knew a bit of Spanish, all she could decipher was "dead" and "princess." This she whispered to Vic.

The Pasos refused to say any more, and Vic begged Jenny to put away the pendant until she returned to Toronto, but she displayed a stubborn streak.

"No, it's mine," she said, "and I'll wear it. If there's a mystery, I want to find out about it. After all, it might prove to be very valuable."

Vic squeezed her hand. "Jenny, I forbid you to wear it."

"Forbid! Oh, don't be a spoilsport." She replied, laughing. And she made no promises.

That night as they slept, Jenny was awakened by a soft sound. She touched Vic, whispering, "There's someone in the room."

Vic jumped up, but by the time he turned on the lights, the intruder had vanished. The dressing table had obviously been tampered with.

"I'm sure they were looking for that pendant," Vic pointed out. "Please, Jenny, don't wear it again. It's bound to bring us trouble."

"Oh, all right. I'll wear my old pendant, but I feel that this one is shrouded in mystery and is probably worth pots of money. I wish I knew all about it, but no one seems to want to talk."

She took the antique from under her pillow, where she had put it when she went to bed, and placed it in her transistor radio in place of the battery. *No one would ever think of looking there,* she guessed.

As they went back to bed, Vic's thoughts were confused and troubled. Jenny consistently spoke of the pendant from a monetary standpoint. The Jenny he knew and loved was not the kind of girl to be enamored of money. Was this a side of her that he was only now discovering? The whole situation bothered him.

Two days later on the bus to Merced—the large marketplace in the vicinity of their boarding house—Jenny noticed a tall slim man staring at her. Later, as they walked through the busy throng of shoppers at the marketplace, she saw the man again. He appeared to be following them.

She kept this observation to herself, but resolved to discover what it was all about. She did not want to bother Vic with it.

Seeing that he was interested in the leather goods, she said, "I'm going over to look at the silver jewelry. Meet me there in half an hour."

She moved off before he could reply, and walked quickly, with the man still behind her. Then she turned on him so swiftly he had no time to retreat. Boldly she asked in slow Spanish, "Why do you follow me?"

He put his hand on her arm and said, "*Venga, senorita.*"

She tried to pull away, but his grip was firm as he pulled her along to a darkened doorway.

There in the dim light she was faced by a rather charming young Mexican, who asked in perfect English, "Where did you get the jade pendant?"

Though frightened, Jenny put on a brave front and retorted, "Find out for yourself."

Unruffled, the man said in an awed tone, "It's beautiful, *senorita,* but do you know what it signifies?"

"No I don't." She was interest now. "Why do you want it?"

"I don't want it, *senorita.* I merely want to know where you got it.

This perplexed Jenny. "Why then did someone break into my room looking for it?"

The handsome dark stranger was puzzled as well, but assured her he knew nothing about that. He had only just been informed of her arrival in Mexico.

Jenny's instincts told her he was speaking the truth, so she decided to be honest. "My father-in-law gave me the pendant. It was in his antique shop in Toronto."

"Please sit down," the man requested, "and I will tell you the story. Have no fear. No harm will come to you."

He took her inside, and once she was seated, he apologized for his associate. "At times my friends become overly emotional when they think they have discovered the genuine pendant, but they would never steal it or hurt you."

He told her he was a Mayan Indian. His name was Jaime Pook, and the Heart of Jade was a very special adornment that the Mayans placed upon their royalty at burial. He related how this particular pendant (from the description he had received, he was sure it was genuine) had not been buried with a Mayan chief—his grandfather—because the chief had given it to his eleven-year-old daughter, Princess Amal, just hours before he died. During the preparations for the chief's burial ceremony, the child had wandered off toward the jungle, and was never seen or heard from again. Some said she had been killed, others that she had been stolen: whoever had done this wanted only to obtain the sacred pendant.

"*Quien sabe?*" he asked. "Who knows?

That princess, he told Jenny, was his aunt. His family had always felt that she was still alive, and they wanted to find her to bring happiness to his grandmother, who still mourned for her. The pendant was their only clue. As an antique, this one was most valuable, for all others were buried with their owners. No wonder someone had tried to steal it. It would bring a fortune to whoever sold it.

The story fascinated Jenny and also made her sad.

Just then they heard heavy footsteps. They jumped up, startled, as two men came in with guns drawn. "Hand over the pendant," one of them ordered Jenny.

Quickly she called out, "I don't have it."

The man went over and grabbed the necklace she was wearing, but soon realized it did not have the pendant on it. "Where is it?" he demanded, shaking her.

"I lost it!"

"You're lying."

Jaime made a move toward her and the man said, "No one tries to leave or he's a dead duck, do you hear?"

Immediately Jenny shouted at the top of her lungs, "Help! Help!"

The man clasped his hand over her mouth. "You do that again and I'll kill you."

Meanwhile, Vic and three policemen were searching frantically for Jenny in the marketplace. They heard her faint cry and hurried over to investigate, bursting into the room. After a scuffle, the two men with guns were subdued and taken into custody.

"All is well, darling. You're safe," Vic comforted Jenny.

After an exchange of explanations, they invited Jaime to supper, where he recounted the tale for Vic's benefit. The only information Vic could offer was that his father had acquired the pendant three years ago from a dealer located at the corner of *Avenida Juarez* and *Calle* Humbolt.

"I hope that helps you a little in locating your missing aunt," he said. "Who knows? She might still be alive."

Just then Jenny leaned over and whispered to her husband, "Do you think your dad would be annoyed if I gave the pendant to Jaime? It rightfully belongs to his family, and though we now know it is worth a fortune as a collector's item, it represents much more to them—more than money can buy. Also it would be restored to its rightful place with his grandfather."

Vic was overcome with emotion at Jenny's display of unselfishness. He kissed her forehead. "Dad would be happy, I'm sure, and I am proud of you."

He realized that his misgivings had been unfounded. All Jenny was guilty of was having a romantic heart; she had never been interested in the pendant for monetary reasons.

Jenny blushed when, on departing with the pendant, Jaime told Vic, "Your wife has worn the Heart of Jade like a true princess of my people. Your generosity will be recorded in our hearts everlastingly."

Almost two weeks later Jenny and Vic were preparing to return to Toronto when Mrs. Pesos knocked on their door, saying they had visitors.

It was Jaime, accompanied by a slender, very beautiful lady with shiny black eyes and long black braids. She was dressed in what they recognized as typical Mayan regalia.

Before anyone could speak, Jenny said, "I knew it. I knew it! This is Princess Amal, isn't it?"

Jaime was all smiles as he introduced his aunt and explained how they had finally found her, making his grandmother happy. "Now," he said, "we want you to come to our village and participate in the welcoming festivities. You'll be treated to a Mayan festival—a celebration you'll never forget."

Vic and Jenny were well pleased. It was a touching finale to their honeymoon.

The Gift

It arrived in the morning mail—an impressive-looking parcel wrapped in brown paper and tied with a double strand of twine. There was nothing to distinguish it from the thousands of other packages passing through the postman's hands every day. But it *was* different—very different.

As he picked up the parcel, Jim said silently between clenched teeth, " Oh, my God, it's come back. What the hell am I going to do now?"

The fact that he could clearly see the post office stamp marked "Moved, Left no forwarding address," presented a real problem for him. He was sorry now that he had stopped to assist the old woman in the shopping plaza last Wednesday, but she had seemed desperate.

At that moment his sister Mary called out, "Are you there, Jim? Open the door, please. I've forgotten my keys again."

Quickly he pushed the parcel into the lower drawer

of his desk, and then went out to help Mary bring in the groceries.

That night as they sat at supper, Mary remarked, "I see from the evening paper that some woman who collapsed in the shopping plaza last week had a package containing a valuable diamond necklace and brooch taken from her while her nephew went for help."

Jim almost choked on the steak he was chewing. *I have to be calm,* he told himself. He hurriedly finished his supper, pushed back his chair and got up. "I'll read about that story later on. Save my dessert, Mary. I just remembered a most important appointment. I've got to run."

It was a shock for him to learn the contents of the package. He felt now that having it in the house was tantamount to keeping a stick of dynamite, and that upset him no end.

Once he got outside, he ran his slender fingers through his curly brown hair and felt like pulling it out in clumps. His brown eyes narrowed almost to slits, seeming darker than the usual hazel, and his shoulders slumped. He plunked down his six-foot slender frame on the wooden bench near the seafront and looked out at the waves splashing on the white, sandy beach.

He sat there for almost an hour, pondering his dilemma. He didn't know if anyone had seen him take the parcel from the woman.

Suddenly an idea occurred to him. He got up and rushed over to the newspaper office, where he placed an ad in the personal column: "Party moved, what next?"

This done, Jim felt better, even though he realized that all he could do now was wait for developments. He

The Gift

hoped it wouldn't take too long.

It had been two weeks and he had lived in constant suspense, because nothing had happened in response to his ad.

Then, in Monday night's paper, it was there: "Tomorrow evening—Ella's, 6 pm."

He knew the restaurant well. Clenching his fists, he silently vowed that not even an earthquake would keep him away from that appointment.

He arrived early and as he sat sipping a lemonade, he recognized her as she walked in the door. She was well dressed in a soft blue suit that accentuated her friendly blue eyes. She was elderly but very elegant. One thought ran through his mind: *she reminds me of my mother.*

The lady came over and asked casually, "May I share your table, young man?"

He got up, pulled out a chair for her, and then proceeded to order coffee for them both.

She came directly to the point, speaking quietly and slowly, her voice cultured though shaking. "I know you're dying of curiosity, so I had better tell you the story."

"Please do," he said, trying to keep the anxiety out of his voice.

"I'm Jennifer Thorne. The necklace and brooch are family heirlooms dating back over 100 years. After my death, they go to my only granddaughter, Marion Thorne. It's she who has moved." Sipping her coffee, Mrs. Thorne paused for a moment before continuing. "That day when I collapsed, I knew that if I lost consciousness, my no-good nephew Thomas, who was with me, would surely steal the package. You see, he knew I had it with me and that I intended to post it to Marion."

She smiled across the table at Jim. "Hence my quick action in asking you to mail it using your return address. She sighed and told him it was a relief to know the package was out of her nephew's reach.

Jim leaned toward her. "You can't imagine how scared I've been these last past few weeks, not knowing what sort of situation I was involved in. You'll have to admit the newspaper left little to my imagination, and I was scared stiff when the parcel was returned."

"Everything was my nephew's doing, the troublemaker."

"Shall I give you the package now?" Jim asked.

"Oh, no," she replied quickly, her well-manicured hands trembling. "Keep it for me, please. You see, my time is very limited. I suffer from a very delicate heart condition and may pop off at any moment. After my death, please hand the parcel over to my lawyers: Brindle and Brindle. I guess you know of them."

Jim was thinking about the value of the parcel. "Yes I do, but you don't even know me."

"True," she said, "but you don't reach my age—I'm 91, you know—without recognizing honesty and reliability in an individual. I'll take my chances on you, but I need your name and address."

As Jim wrote it down and handed the paper to her, she laughed as she looked at it. "Well, James Denning, in any event, if anything unforeseen happens, I would rather you got the jewels than my nephew, Thomas Blaine."

Mrs. Thorne stood. "Now I *must* go or they'll be wondering where I've been and what I've been up to. They don't trust me, you know."

Jim came around and offered to walk her to wherever she was going.

"Thanks, my boy," she said, "for helping out a stranger. You won't regret it." She took both his hands and squeezed them firmly. "Please call a taxi for me. I must go now. Rest assured, you have nothing to fear."

Almost two months later the letter arrived. Mary had to sign for it because it was registered. Upon opening it and reading the contents, Jim was so flabbergasted that he couldn't speak. He merely handed it over to Mary and then sat down, trying to collect his scattered thoughts.

The letter stated that Mrs. Thorne had died a month earlier, and that her will stipulated: "When James Denning hands over to my lawyers, Brindle and Brindle, the parcel I have entrusted to his care, he is to receive the sum of $10,000."

Her dark eyes large as saucers, Mary sat back and asked, "Is this for real?"

"I guess so, though it is so totally unexpected that I'm stunned. I have the parcel here in my drawer." He thought with sadness of the old lady he had helped, and wondered what the outcome would be if Mrs. Thorne's nephew decided to come claim the package or even try to rob their house. He hoped Thomas Blaine knew nothing of the letter Jim had just received.

He said to Mary, "Please come with me to the lawyer's office right now. I want to hand over the parcel right away. I'm too scared to keep it any longer. It's extremely valuable and actually belongs to Mrs. Thorne's granddaughter. She told me her nephew would do anything to get his hands on it."

In the lawyer's office Jim and Mary sat facing the elderly Mr. Tom Brindle. Jim handed him the parcel and signed the form acknowledging that Mr. Brindle had placed it in the wall safe right away.

"Now," he said, "I have a cheque for $10,000 for you."

"Oh, no you don't," said a voice from the doorway.

It was Thomas Blaine.

"Either you make that cheque out to me, or give me the parcel," he demanded.

"Mr. Blaine," Mr. Brindle informed him, "the parcel is already well secured, and it is not yours. Neither is the cheque. Please leave my office."

Thomas went over to the elderly lawyer, staring him in the eyes, and said roughly, "Either I get what I want or no one leaves this room alive."

Mary and Jim were shaking in their shoes, but Mr. Brindle, apparently unafraid, refused quite firmly. "Mr. Blaine, your aunt's will stipulates that you are to receive $50,000 on two conditions. These are that you leave this city and never return, and that you never contact any of your family for any reason for the next ten years. I have a form for you to sign to that effect."

Thomas jerked back, startled. "Is that true? Did she actually leave me $50,000?"

"Yes," replied Mr. Brindle, "but remember, it has conditions attached."

"I can live with that."

"Well then, please wait outside until I finish my business withy Mr. Denning."

Very subdued, Thomas went outside and sat down. He

thought he had gotten off easily because he only owed about $5,000. The rest of the money would be handy for his use, and he never really cared to see his family anyhow. None of them but his aunt had money; he'd only tolerated her because of that.

As for Jim and Mary, they were relieved to know Mrs. Thorne's affairs were now settled. As they left the office, they were trying to decide whether to buy a new car or take a trip to Hawaii.

The Man

It was a blistering hot day. Jane leaned her slender body against the tree and blinked her brown eyes as she wiped the sweat from her face. Her brown curls hung limply on her shoulders. She wiped her neck and brushed her hair back.

Suddenly she stood still as she focused on the man sauntering towards her. He moved effortlessly, and she thought, *what a gait!* His torso was erect like a rake and his tawny tousled hair fell over his furrowed forehead in a riot of waves. Steel blue eyes stared at Jane hypnotically from under bushy eyebrows.

They seemed to be willing her to say something, or even to smile, but Jane was no weakling where men were concerned. She held her ground and uttered not a word; her face was blank and unimpressed. She felt mesmerized, yet she sensed danger in the air. She had heard of this person but had never seen him or met him. She had no desire to do so now. Actually she felt

The Man

like running away.

Pressing his thin lips into a tight line, and with a gentle swing of his lean hips, he passed nearby. Jane could feel his breath and his magnetism. Ever so softly, he whispered in passing, "Be seeing you, sweetheart." Then he looked her straight in the eyes.

Suddenly she felt naked and it irritated her that this man could be so bold as to undress her with his eyes. She was sure he was aware of his effect on her. "I'll see you in hell," she replied from between clenched teeth as she turned and walked away.

Running his hand through his hair, his laughter rang out as he said loudly, "That's what they all say, my darling." And he continued walking.

Jane had heard stories about this man and she had no intention of falling under his spell. She thought he was sadistic, for she had heard how his wife had left him after he tried to tie her nude under an ant-infested tree. He had also buried his baby daughter alive once because, or so he said, "That damn infant cries too much. It irritates me." Fortunately his wife got someone to unearth the child before it suffocated. The stories were endless. Eventually the wife divorced him.

On reaching home, Jane phoned her friend, Ann, and related the incident to her. "Who the hell does he think he is?" asked Jane.

"King of Women, of course," Ann replied. "Surely you know of him?"

"Yes, I've heard of him but never seen him before. Is he really as terrible as people make out?"

Ann said, "Indeed he is. But now he only comes to town once a week, and then his eyes may fancy some new girl. You appear to be the target this time."

"Well this girl will be his downfall, I assure you."

Ann was unconvinced. "You ooze with personality, my dear, and your attitude this evening offers a great challenge to him, I'm sure."

Jane shook her head. "He'd best forget he ever saw me, or he'll live to regret it," she said with great emphasis.

"We'll see, we'll see. No one he fancies has ever escaped him yet," Ann pointed out.

Jane was so annoyed she almost shouted, "This one will! This one will!"

The next evening as she was leaving work, she noticed him leaning against the wall outside the liquor store nearby. She pretended not to see him and hailed a passing taxi to take her home. As the taxi drove off, she saw him throw his cigarette down and stamp his foot. It was clear she had thwarted him and he was annoyed. The expression on his face frightened her. She was cold and afraid. She decided to phone her Aunt Millie and ask her about the man.

Her aunt told Jane a horrible tale.

Marco O'Boyle was the man's name. Ever since he was a teenager, he'd been known as the terror of the area. He had raped girls, though nothing could be proven against him, for the girls were too terrified to testify, in case he victimized them or their family later. Even the men were fearful of him; he took their farm animals and mutilated them whenever he felt like it. The men were afraid for their families, because Marco was known to move as softly as a cat.

"In other words," Jane said to her Aunt Millie, "this

man does as he likes and everyone sits by and does nothing to stop him."

"Yes, that's the picture."

Jane straightened her shoulders. "Well he won't do what he likes with me. He's a bully and I won't tolerate his kind."

This frightened her aunt. "Please be careful, my child. Don't cross Marco. He's very dangerous," she warned. "Just keep out of his way."

"He's sick in the head, that's what," Jane replied.

But Aunt Millie was worried. She knew Jane was strong-willed—and so was Marco.

The next day as Jane worked in the post office, she could see Marco outside walking up and down. Occasionally he'd look in and stare at her, but he didn't come in. She asked to go home early and left by the side door, again taking a taxi.

At home that night she spoke to Ann, who told her, "Marco is raving mad. He waited until 5:00 p.m., and when you didn't come out from work, he knew you'd foiled him again."

"So what, I don't know him and I don't want to."

Ann sighed before giving a warning. "Please, Jane, be very careful of that man. He is determined to have you."

That night Jane slept on the kitchen floor with a knife by her side. She was really beginning to be frightened.

The next morning on her way to work, Marco stepped into her path and said, "Hello, Jane."

She looked at him with disdain. "Good morning."

"May I walk you home later?" he asked very politely.

"No, thank you. I'm dining out with friends."

"Well, tomorrow then?" he asked, smiling in a smug way.

"No, not tomorrow or ever," Jane told him, and walked off quickly.

"You'll regret it," he shouted after her.

Jane turned, looking him straight in the eyes. "Now, you listen to me. I don't go out with sadists or rapists."

He turned very red in the face and replied angrily, "You'll beg me to love you yet. I'll see to it."

Frightened that she had said too much, she quickly walked on, listening to his laughter behind her. Then she heard him say loudly,

"You and I will have such a good time loving, we'll collapse with exhaustion, and I know you'll beg for more. Maybe I'll consent, and then maybe I won't. We'll see."

That night when Jane got home, she telephoned her cousin, John, the cop she saw only at Christmas when the family gathered together in the next town. She tried to explain her dilemma and told him her fears. She was very agitated. It was fortunate that Ann had told her Marco had returned to his farm that evening. This was a small town where everyone knew what went on.

"Does Marco appeal to you as a man?" John asked.

"Yes," she admitted slowly, "he's got such animal magnetism, it's frightening, but I know it's only that. I actually detest his type; he's a rapist and a sadist. I would rather kill myself than love him."

"We'll have to think of something," John mused, "or you may have to move from the area."

Jane took a deep breath. "I guess so."

The problem was that Marco knew he had charm. He no doubt was an excellent lover, but that was all he was good for because he was really wicked, thoughtless and had no conscience; he was extremely selfish. "The man is a selfish heel, born with an ideal body and the charm of a snake," Jane said. "No wonder girls won't talk against him. They love him and hate him at the same time."

"What do you suggest I do to help?" John asked.

"Well, you *are* a cop, and no one knows you around here," Jane suggested. "No one knows we are related. Get a couple of days off next week when Marco is in town and we'll take it from there. What do you think?"

John agreed. I'm due for some time off. I'll talk to you tomorrow and we'll see what we can come up with. Bye for now."

With that Jane had to be content.

On the weekend, John came to town and surprised her. He accompanied her to work Monday morning and picked her up at 5:00. Marco was leaning against the wall outside, and when they passed, he said, "Hi, Jane. That boyfriend will do you no good. I'm the one you need to teach you how to love. See you later."

John tightened his hold on Jane's hand and whispered, "Ignore him."

Was Money the Issue?

It appeared to be a very nice party. People were well dressed and there seemed to be a happy, joyous atmosphere. Mary was late and, as she entered the crowded room, she looked across to where John was standing alone with a wineglass in his hand. He was looking rather absently out the window. She knew that when they met, he would expect her to fall into his arms as usual, yet she noted that his handsome face had a rather distant look. He was tastefully dressed in grey, which brought out the green highlights in his eyes. His brown hair was well cut and smooth. She admired his erect, slender figure.

She wondered if he too had fallen in love with someone else while she was away. Maybe he too had found someone with lots of cash. "I hope, for his sake, that

Was Money the Issue?

she's pretty too. I really like John; he's very elegant and I want him to be happy," she said to herself while she stood looking at him. As she walked over, she said softly, "Hello, John, how are you doing?"

He turned (was it eagerly, she wondered?) and murmured, "Hello, Mary," putting out his hands to greet her.

She did not take them but hesitated. "I have something to tell you." Then she added hurriedly, "I've fallen in love with someone else. I met him in New York. I'm sorry."

John's greenish eyes turned dark as he looked into Mary's blue ones. Then he said slowly, "I know we can't control the wanderings of our hearts and our emotions. If you think this person will make you happy, I am content. It's what you want that counts, at least to me." He touched her cheek affectionately. "I hope he knows you are a jewel and that he treats you tenderly."

Mary brushed her auburn hair back with her hand and slipped the ring from her finger. "Here's your ring, John. I'm terribly sorry. I never meant to hurt you.

He took it from her. "I wish you every happiness. If you find you need a friend though, I am always here for you." He embraced her and kissed her cheek.

She could feel him tremble. It was then she realized that he had not fallen in love with someone else. She hadn't meant to hurt him, she kept telling herself, but she hadn't realized how deeply he loved her. Silently, she said, *At least I'm glad he doesn't realize how shallow I am and that money is the thing that matters most to me.*

She had spent many nights thinking there was no way

she could ever live on John's small technician's salary. *If only I didn't have such expensive tastes. A pity love has to get in the way.*

Riding an Elephant

Have you ever ridden an elephant? I mean really ridden one? Not in one of those fancy seats, like a Sultan or some important visitor to India or Pakistan. You know the kind of thing I mean: a soft, cushioned seat—well padded so you feel as if you are in your easy chair by the fireplace—but this chair is perched high up in the air and you can turn your head and view the countryside as you please, or close your eyes and imagine you are floating on a cloud.

That is not, by any stretch of the imagination, really riding an elephant. Why, you miss all the fun and excitement. I shall tell you about my experience. It was an unforgettable episode in my life, believe me.

One night I talked cheerfully to a little Indian boy on

many topics, and foolishly divulged my great and burning desire to ride an elephant. The next morning he called me early.

As I left the house, he tugged at my slacks, saying, "Come on, Mrs. Mandin, the elephant is here."

I gulped with shock when I saw looming over me a massive brown elephant that was eyeing me quite directly, as if to say, "Don't tell me you're scared of little old me?"

I looked up, seeking the comfortable seat I had visualized as the proper and only way in which to ride an elephant, but all I saw was a flimsy cloth, which Saba, the Indian boy, assured me was a blanket. Take my advice, folks, don't ever be misled by the pictures you see in advertisements about elephant rides. "Where's the seat?" I inquired.

"Seat, why, Mrs. Mandin, don't you want to ride the elephant?"

"Sure, Saba," I replied. By now I wished my husband and I had left the night before, and that I had not been so willing to voice my secret ambition to the boy.

"Well then, what do you need a seat for? Come along," he said, dragging me by the hand. "Zum is ready."

That, I presumed, was the name of the mountain of flesh. Just then my husband appeared and said laughingly, "That's a nice big one, eh? Come on, you've finally got your wish."

By this time, the elephant was kneeling in readiness for me to mount. I looked around hopefully for a last chance to wriggle out of this predicament, when Saba dashed my hopes by saying, "Surely you are not afraid, Mrs. Mandin?"

Riding an Elephant

That did it. If it killed me, I would ride that elephant. I couldn't let the child think I was a coward. He would think all foreigners were cowards. If the truth were told, I was pretty scared, though.

Saba's father had appeared on the scene by this time, and he helped me up, telling me to be sure and hold the ropes. I hung on to those ropes for dear life. With the flimsy cloth under me, I slid first to the left, then to the right. I was sure I would fall off and Zum would trample me.

Eventually I managed to keep myself steady. Then it happened.... The elephant began to rise. Naturally she unfolded her front feet first, and I felt myself sliding backwards. I was sure I would slide down her tail until I realized I was still hanging on to the ropes. Boy, did I hang on!

As the huge mountain of flesh rose to full height, I slid in all directions: right, left, backwards—never forward. It was like being in a tiny rowboat in a heavy storm on rough seas. I was sure I felt seasick, but I didn't really.

Then I discovered I was steady at last. Yes! Zum trotted around slowly; she must have been used to nervous, frightened riders, for she moved ever so carefully. It felt a bit queer at first, being up so high, almost as if I was on top of the world and rocking in the wind. I could see all around me, and as I got used to the sensation and over the initial shock, I found I was actually enjoying myself. It gave me quite a thrill.

I can assure you that I never, for one fraction of a second, let go of the ropes, for I had the unconscious fear of suddenly losing my balance and sliding off. But believe me, now that it is over, I wouldn't have missed the experience.

So unless you ride an elephant bareback, never say, "I've ridden an elephant"; for indeed, you really have not. Try it and see for yourself.

A Cup of Happiness

At 23 years old, Ann Bowers felt that life was passing her by. *Life is so monotonous,* she thought. Trudging along the lonely road, a half-mile from the bus stop to her home, her thoughts were as gloomy and dull as the day had been. "I guess I'm just bored," she mused." Then her thoughts turned to Johnny Lands. Here she permitted herself to dream a little. How nice it would be if Johnny paid attention to her. Yet somehow Ann felt he preferred her friend, Marie Spencer. "They are probably together right now," she said out loud.

Ann always had been a trifle envious of Marie. In her view, Marie was pretty, tall, assured and glamorous—unlike herself. She was quiet and unsophisticated. Ann didn't realize that she was a startling beauty with her slender fingers, sleek brown hair, grayish eyes, full sensuous lips, and a smile to light up a room and turn the head of any stranger. She always felt dowdy when she compared herself to other people. She didn't recognize her assets and potential.

Marie often gave Ann the impression that Johnny had taken her to exotic restaurants, the opera, and other diversions. Ann sometimes wondered if Marie made it all up, for all three were good friends, and it was unlike Johnny to single out one of them. But she dared not ask him in case it was all true. For Ann the highlights in her life were when all three of them walked together in the park or watched videos at home. She felt so happy then.

After supper that night, as she and her father sat in the living room, Ann was attracted by an advertisement in the local paper. She burst out, "Oh, Dad, look! Baliff Airlines is holding a beauty and intelligence contest. The prize is a Caribbean cruise for two weeks. Gosh! I would so love to win that."

Closing her eyes for a moment, she sighed dreamily and uttered a silent prayer.

Her father had been deeply engrossed in his archeological work since the death of his wife some years ago. He failed to detect the wishful note in his daughter's voice. Carelessly, he said, "That's not for you, my pet. It's for glamour girls."

Ann felt deflated, but nevertheless continued, "But I have to try at least. I think I *will* apply and see what happens."

"Go ahead, my dear, and good luck," Mr. Bowers responded absently as he continued his work—and immediately forgot all about the conversation.

"How wonderful if I should win," Ann whispered to

herself, "and I do have two weeks vacations due me at the office." She visualized what it would be like to travel to foreign places and have all the expenses paid. "I could never afford such a wonderful trip, but, oh! It would be so marvelous."

Her eyes looked dreamy in her heart-shaped face, and she wriggled her classically aquiline nose as she got up to get her pen so she could answer the intelligence questions in the paper. "I'm sure I can win this part of the contest; that's the first hurdle. I will think about the beauty part afterwards," she said to herself as she started.

Just as she finished later that evening, she heard the "toot", "toot" of Marie's car—or rather, Mr. Spencer's car. She rushed outside all agog with excitement. "Marie! Marie, have you read about the contest?"

Marie, who never bothered to read the papers, replied in an offhand tone, "No, tell me about it."

Of course she was very interested, but tried not to show it. The year before she had won a local beauty pageant, and ever since then, she felt she could conquer anything. Lowering her greenish eyes, she said offhandedly, "I'd love to try, just for the fun of it, of course." Inwardly she felt Ann hadn't a ghost of a chance. Marie's imagination ran wild as she contemplated the many rich, handsome young men she would meet on the cruise. She hoped one would ask her to marry him.

Just then Johnny, who lived nearby, passed. He was curious to know what the girls were so excited about. He worked in the same law office where Ann was a stenographer.

"Oh, Johnny," the girls chorused, "there's a beauty contest on at Baliff Airlines, and the winner will get a trip to the Caribbean for two whole weeks, all expenses paid. Just think of it."

"You'll both enter, I presume," he said, and for some unknown reason, as he looked at Ann's flushed face, so keen with excitement and anticipation, he felt he wanted her to win. Then the thought struck him suddenly, *What if she meets some man on the cruise and falls in love?* He considered Ann to be a sweet girl, and thought she deserved the best, but he couldn't understand why he felt it wouldn't matter much if Marie met someone and got married.

Of course he didn't know that Marie considered him her property, at least until someone better showed up.

Marie worked as a typist in an office just half a block away from the Baliff Airlines office, so she said to Ann, "I can easily drop your entry off on my way to work in the morning if you get it ready now, and it will save you the time and bother."

Ann was so pleased at this burst of kindness from the usually selfish Marie that she had no misgivings, and later that evening, she handed her envelope to her friend.

Two weeks later as the girls sat in "Tony's" having ice cream after work, Marie looked up. "Oh, here's Johnny."

He came towards them and, in taking up Marie's large handbag from the vacant chair so he could sit down, the bag dropped, spilling the contents.

Marie hastily tried to gather up everything: papers, lipstick, compact, tissues, and other little items scattered on the floor. But Ann's eye caught a familiar envelope.

She exclaimed, "Why, Marie, you haven't put in my entry for the contest yet, and the deadline is today."

Marie flushed deeply, but thought quickly and said

hastily, "Oh my goodness, I do believe I have handed in the wrong envelope. I'm so sorry, Ann."

Johnny had a puzzled look but said calmly, "Let's go right away to the airline office and deliver it."

Marie could think of no objection, so off they went, yet she kept thinking. "You never know; those judges might be taken in by Ann's innocent look. I would hate for her to win."

By this time, Johnny had begun to look at her in a new light. He wondered whether she had deliberately refused to turn in Ann's envelope. He knew Marie was vain and selfish, but he thought the girls were good friends, and he did like them both. Again, for some reason he could not explain, he had a longing to protect Ann, yet he could not understand why. He knew he didn't trust Marie. He never had. *I wonder what Ann thinks of me? He mused, I know I'm just an ordinary guy who is quite tall, has brown hair, black eyes, and a straight nose. I have a determined mouth, but Ann is so interested in this contest, I doubt she notices me as a person. Why should she, anyway? But I do love to see her eyes light up when she's excited.*

Ann, honest person that she was, said to Marie as they walked back, "How fortunate that Johnny overturned your handbag and we discovered the mistake in time."

"Yes indeed," Marie replied.

Not for one moment did Ann entertain the thought that Marie would not want her to enter the contest; Ann didn't consider herself competition for her friend in any case, but thought she had a slim chance. At least she wanted to have entered and lost, rather than not to have tried at all.

Two nights later as she sat at supper, she was so thrilled she hardly ate, because on arriving home, she had received a special delivery letter, notifying her that she should be at City Hall at 5:00 p.m., room 101, tomorrow for the beauty pageant.

Even her father came to life for once and kissed her forehead when she read the letter to him. He did warn her, "Don't bank on it too much, my dear, though I would love for you to win. Good luck!"

Marie telephoned at that moment and said in a bubbling voice, "I've received a latter, Ann. I'm in the contest."

Excitedly, Ann responded, "I got a letter too."

For a while there was silence. Finally Ann asked, "Are you still there, Marie?"

Hiding her disappointment, Marie offered sweetly, "I'll come over and take you to my hairdresser. She'll fix you up beautifully to show your best points. Then it's a case of 'may the best girl win', eh?"

Unsuspecting, Ann agreed.

Later that evening at the hairdresser, Ann was persuaded to cut her tresses, and though her hair curled beautifully around her head, giving her face a most intriguing look, when they were outside, Marie told her it looked awful.

This distressed Ann and broke her confidence. She felt miserable and hardly spoke on the way home, but Marie prattled on cheerfully, even offering to come and pick her friend up the next day to go to City Hall.

As she drove off, she felt satisfied as she smiled to herself. "With Ann's state of mind, she might not even want to appear tomorrow, *if* she gets there at all," she said quietly to the wind.

At 4:00 the next day, Ann was ready, but by 4:15, when Marie failed to turn up, Ann felt jittery. At 4:30 she realized Marie was not coming, and of course Ann had no car. At that hour, taxis were nonexistent. "Surely if something had happened, Marie would have telephoned."

Ann argued with herself, willing, as usual, to give her friend the benefit of the doubt. She was downhearted and forlorn. She felt like crying. She tried Marie's number, but her mother answered, saying she had left long ago.

Ann now realized Marie was a traitor and had been deliberately sabotaging her friend from the beginning. Woodenly she dialed Johnny's number. She had to tell someone. She breathed a sigh of relief when he answered, and haltingly told him, "I'm stranded, Johnny, and the contest is at 5:00 today. Marie did offer to pick me up, but she has not come. Her mother said she left an hour ago. I don't think she'll come."

Johnny was extremely angry. He realized, just as Ann had, that Marie was out only for herself. He took a deep, determined breath. "Be at your gate. I'll get you there in time." He recalled that his next-door neighbor's son had an old motorbike, and though it had been years since he had ridden one, he intended to borrow it now. In a flash he also realized that he was in love with Ann and that was why he hated to see her hurt and disappointed, or taken advantage of.

He picked her up within five minutes, and though she had never ridden on a motorbike before, she was not afraid with Johnny. She hung onto him for dear life.

They went so fast that when they had almost reached the intersection a block from City Hall, a traffic cop whizzed up and stopped them. Johnny whispered to Ann, "You can just make it if you walk fast. You look like a million dollars and I'm confident you'll win, my darling. See you later.

Ann slipped off the bike and walked quickly in the direction of City Hall. She reached it just as the contestants were filing in, and quietly took her place. Marie led the group, looking gorgeous in green, but in her simply cut light blue dress with a full skirt, Ann felt on top of the world as she remembered Johnny's parting words: *my darling.*

She stood tall—all of her five-feet-eight inches. Her face was glowing as she walked across the platform.

The judges watched her intently, and one whispered to the other, "That one is outstanding. The beauty of the soul shines in her face." Another judge said, "That girl has real natural beauty which comes from within and shows outside." They were not long in deliberating; Ann was pronounced the winner.

Just then Johnny came in. He went up to where the judges were talking to her. He said, "I'm so glad she won, but two weeks is a long time to wait for someone you love." He looked at her tenderly.

She couldn't believe her ears. She turned shining eyes to him and he held her hands tightly and squeezed them. As they left the building, Marie swung past them and hissed, ""I hope the ship runs into a storm."

But Ann was so happy she could afford to feel sorry for Marie. "Your turn will come, Marie. Just be patient."

A Cup of Happiness

Marie stalked off.

Ann looked lovingly into Johnny's face and he kissed her. "I'll wait for you until you get back. I'll sure miss you, though, and please don't ever change."

Ann replied, "I won't; I promise." She leaned into his arms, "Oh, Johnny, I not only won a contest and a cruise, I also fell in love and am loved in return. I'm so happy. My cup of happiness is full."

The Day the World Stood Still

The air was motionless. Not a leaf was stirring. A calm existed that felt like liquid stillness permeating the atmosphere and enveloping everything. Even the birds sitting on the tree branches resembled tiny robots left by some extraterrestrial being.

Mike sat on a boulder in the clearing and ran his fingers through his tousled black hair as he gazed at his surroundings. He wished he knew what to do. He was in a daze and shook his head as if to clear his mind.

The Day the World Stood Still

He felt that he was the only human being left on the planet. It was awful being stuck in the middle of nowhere on the mountainside. As Mike looked around, there seemed to be no path leading out as far as he could see. He felt utterly helpless.

"All I wanted was a peaceful vacation," he said out loud, "but definitely not this eerie stillness."

It wasn't peaceful; it was frightening.

When Mike left home that morning, he had been happy and carefree and looking forward with great anticipation to the drive along the hillside road. He was humming and thought he would just go wherever the road led him. After all, he had a week's vacation and just wanted to relax.

Now here he was, suspended as if in space. Sure, it had been an accident, but now what? His Toyota had been thrown over and over, ending upside-down in the clearing.

He blinked his brown eyes and began to reflect. *Let me reconstruct the accident,* he thought to himself.

One minute he had been driving along the road, quite carefree, and suddenly, within the blink of an eye, the wind seemed to gain a huge velocity that shook his car like a cat shaking a mouse it has just caught. Within seconds he was hurled down the mountainside.

He was positive it had not been a tornado. When he crawled out of his car, even his clothes were unwrinkled and he was unhurt. Actually, he felt wonderful.

"This is really weird," he said. "It is as if I was not in an accident at all." Nevertheless, he could see his car was upside-down and definitely dented.

He stood up and looked around carefully. It was then

he saw the tiny object that looked like a ring. He walked over and bent to pick it up, but found it was attached to something large and heavy. He tugged and tugged until it lifted.

It was a trap door. There were steps leading down, and he discerned a very bright light at the bottom.

Mike hesitated. He looked around again and then decided he would take a chance and go down the stairs. Very gingerly he took one step at a time. All was so very still, he could almost hear himself think.

At the bottom of the stairs was a huge room, brilliantly lit, although he could see no actual visible light fixtures. In the center of the room was a dais with shimmering stars at the edges and a tall golden structure, like a lighthouse, in the center.

Mike shivered and stood where he was. No one seemed be in the room, but he sensed a presence. "Hello!" he shouted. "Is anyone there?"

There was absolute silence.

He stepped inside and peered around. He was so frightened that his legs felt numb. Then, as if out of thin air, a man stood before him. He was extremely handsome and looked like a Greek god, with flawless bronzed skin; piercing blue eyes that seemed to look right through him; thick curly hair; a straight nose; and a sensuous mouth. Mike felt small and insignificant as he gazed at this creature, who seemed to glow.

The man bowed slightly and said, "I am Dromedon. Are you from this dimension?"

He seems friendly enough, Mike thought. "Dimension?" he asked, startled.

"Yes, this is Dimension Two," the man replied. "I can see you have never heard of us."

"No," Mike replied, "but how could I be here? All I had was an accident in my car."

"What's a car?" Dromedon asked.

"Come, I'll show you," Mike offered, anxious to get back outside. He led the way back up the stairs to the clearing.

Dromedon looked at the car, then, with a wave of his hand, the car turned back up on its four wheels. All the dents were gone and the paint was shiny. It looked practically new.

Mike was astonished.

Then Dromedon put his hands over his eyes as if to shade them from the sun. "Come," he said, "I cannot be in sunlight too long or I will evaporate." With that he beckoned for Mike to follow him back down the stairs. I have to be prepared for your dimension," he explained.

As they went down, Dromedon asked, "What is your name? Are there others like you?"

Mike told him there were millions, even billions like him.

"What do you do?" the other man asked.

Mike explained that they worked, played, had families, and even spoke different languages. He said they traveled to many countries but never to other dimensions.

"I would like to go to your dimension," Dromedon said. "May I? I could stay only a very short while."

"Do come along," Mike replied. "But how will we get back to my dimension?"

"Leave that to me," Dromedon said. "Close your eyes and touch the dais."

Mike closed his eyes and placed his hands where he

was told. When he opened them, he was on the hillside road in his car, alone, driving and being flagged down by a stranger. He did not remember having an accident. He stopped, and though the person looked familiar, he could not remember ever meeting him.

"Where are you going?" Mike asked.

The man replied, "I am a stranger, and lost. I recently arrived in town. Can you give me a lift?"

The man was very well dressed and handsome, and he did remind Mike of someone he had either met or dreamed about. "What's your name?" he inquired.

"Dromedon," the man said. "I'm on a visit for only a day. Could you maybe show me around?"

Mike said he would be delighted.

Dromedon was a nice, well-educated person with a pleasing personality. He asked many questions and was intensely curious about so many things, it was as if he was from another planet.

That night they checked into a motel, and early the next day, took off in Mike's car to explore the country-side. By nightfall they were really bushed and turned in early.

Mike awoke early the following morning. When his friend did not appear for breakfast, he went and knocked on his door. The cleaning lady, in the hallway, told Mike that the man had checked out at around 4 a.m.

She said, "I think he left something for you at the front desk."

Mike went immediately to the front desk, where the receptionist handed him a small package which, when opened, held a replica of the dais in the underground room. He looked at it intently, trying to understand what it meant. He knew he had seen it somewhere...but where? Had he dreamed it?

As he sat in the lobby in pensive thought, he looked outside and saw Dromedon standing as he looked in the underground room. He waved goodbye to Mike, then seemed to evaporate before his eyes. Then it struck him. Yes, he was sure he'd had an accident.

But, can I explain it to anyone, he thought.

He knew now that he had gone to another dimension, but how could he mention the experience to anyone? No one would believe him. They would think he was nuts. He decided to keeps things to himself, but he prized the gift from Dromedon.

As the years went by, Mike eventually married. As he became older, he often thought he saw his friend, Dromedon, but he always seemed to evaporate before Mike could talk with him. It was as if he had met his guardian angel, which kept constant watch over him.

He often told his grandchildren about the day he had an accident when the world stood still, and that there were other dimensions that did exist, though it was only by accident that one crossed into that world.

Mike was sure it had not been a dream, and in any case, he had a souvenir to prove the fact. Besides, Dromedon visited him often, though they never conversed.

What Mike didn't know was that the replica Dromedon had given him possessed certain powers. It was Mike's son who accidentally discovered this fact.

The Dominant Twin

Bob looked up and saw Marc coming towards him, carrying his briefcase. He stopped what he was doing and asked, "Where are you going at this time of day? Has something happened?"

Marc replied, "I'm heading for home."

"Why? Are you sick or something?" asked Bob again.

"No," Marc snapped, "but I am tired of working, so I've just quit."

"Quit?" said Bob. "What about your family?"

"They'll be fine, I'm sure, but I am fed up with working for a living, so I'm leaving. Goodbye." With that, he headed towards the gate.

Bob shook his head as if to clear his mind, because he didn't understand the conversation he'd just had. It didn't make sense. He turned to his co-worker, Jon, and said, "Marc *must* be ill. He has a good job here in the construction business, he has a lovely wife and daughter to support; why would he just up and quit? Something must have happened. There has to be a reason."

Before Jon could reply, Bob shouted after Marc, "You'll keep in touch, won't you?"

Without even turning his head, Marc gave a backward wave of his hand and replied, "Oh, sure," and walked through the gate.

Jon and Bob discussed the situation as they continued working. Both knew Marc's wife worked, but then Jon said, "He always said they needed both salaries to make ends meet, especially since his daughter is only 12 years old."

"Quite true, his job keeps him away from home a lot of the time. We only go home every two months for a week or so, but Marc is always talking about his great love for his family," said Bob.

"I know," replied Jon. "You know how fed up we can get sometimes when he rambles on about them."

Another worker nearby remarked, "It must be something to do with the letter he received this morning. Could it be bad news? Maybe his wife left him."

Bob smiled and said, "If that had happened, we would have heard. As you know, Marc loves to talk, and he can't keep any news to himself, good or bad. He gets so excited."

Then Jon said, "It must be something to do with his twin sister. They are very close-knit."

"Oh, yes," said Bob. "From conversations, I have wondered how he managed to break away from her and get married."

"Quite true," said Jon. "Now I recall him telling me about her. He always seemed to be in awe of her. I believe she has a lot of money; he was always talking about all her great possessions."

"That must be it," they all agreed. "We'll just have to wait and see." They went back to work.

It was the day after Marc had arrived at his sister's home, where he had headed upon leaving his job. He was sitting in the armchair outside and kept running his pudgy fingers like a comb through his light brown hair. He seemed more nervous than usual, and his grey eyes seemed sad behind the thick lenses he wore. Nevertheless, he said out loud, "This is the life for me. No more hustling and rushing around to make a buck, no one to tell me what to do and when to do it."

He yawned slowly, then sort of heaved himself out of the chair; his 190 pounds were burdensome, though he refused to admit it. He always told his co-workers that his wife was a nag about his weight. Now he said, "Well, Berna, my dear, you won't have to be concerned about my size and eating habits anymore." He pressed his lips together tightly and said between his teeth, "I can eat anything I want now and not be limited."

Just then Bess, his twin sister, came up the path. Smilingly, she said to him, "How are things, Marc? Enjoying yourself?"

"Oh, yes indeed, Sis," he replied, yawning again. "It's so good to be here. I feel so free, and I don't have to work. It's really heavenly to be able to get up when I want, eat what I want, have no wife to ask me to do this or that, no daughter to harass me, no mother-in-law to bug me. This is the life for me."

Marc and Bess always got on well together; they had been inseparable since birth, though Bess had always been the leader. Except she had always let him think he was having his own way. She was quite devious.

He leaned against the door and yawned again, but his eyes looked sad and weary, and his expression revealed a conflict between two worlds. Bess ignored all this as she always ignored things when she wanted her own way. "I told you it was the right thing to come be here with me."

She had been lonesome since Len, her husband of twenty-one years, had died of a heart attack three months ago. She was sure that Marc would fill that gap now he was here. Though she'd loved Len, she had missed Marc terribly after she got married. Actually, she didn't care whether her brother's wife missed Marc, or whether her twin was having second thoughts about accepting her offer. She knew he was here and she intended to keep him with her.

Len had left Bess well provided for, and this was her reason for writing to Marc at his workplace, telling him that he need never work again if he decided to come live with her. She knew he had a lazy streak in him and she had never really considered him married, so she felt no guilt about her actions. She had resented his marriage and ignored it as much as she could without letting him know it.

"It's so nice to have you here with me," she told her brother. "Just like old times, eh?" She knew that after she married Len, he had gone off immediately to another city and married Berna, who she thought was rather young for him, though quite independent. Bess felt that he did what he did in defiance, because he had resented her marriage. At her wedding, everyone had commented on how sulky Marc was. Through the years, both their marriages had hung like a thick cobweb of resentment between them, though they never once discussed the subject.

Marc had spent many vacations with Len and his sister, mainly because she begged him to come and knew he couldn't refuse her anything. Len and he had become good friends, and all three had developed a strong bond of friendship and got on well together. Bess thought to herself, *Funny how I never could bring myself to like Marc's wife. She took him away from me, really.*

Bess had been telling her brother this in many subtle ways on the various occasions when he visited her and brought his wife and daughter along. She often said, "Your wife doesn't seem to love you the way I love Len. She doesn't make a fuss over you the way I do over Len." She always pointed out the comparisons very emphatically.

Marc tried to make excuses for Berna, but his twin simply laughed them off, saying, "Oh, come on, Marc, surely you realize she only tolerates you." Bess was such a strong character, and Marc was the opposite: a weakling, always in her shadow.

Eventually, Marc began to notice and judge everything his wife did. He had become almost paranoid. He had always been extremely sensitive about love and attention. Always after a visit to his sister, he began to demand more and more attention from Berna, and was quite irritated if she didn't seem over-eager to cater to his demands. He put it down to being rejected and unloved. Yet he was quite insensitive to his wife's needs. He never expected her to be tired or have problems at her job. In his view, whatever she said or did was always aimed directly at him, because she probably didn't love him.

On his last trip home with his family, he began demanding a 24-hour demonstration of love from his wife and daughter. Bess's barbs had struck such a note with him that he was paranoid to a point where often Berna would get upset with him. He always had to be the centre of attraction, always having to hold the floor like a politician.

This trait often embarrassed his wife, as did his constant talk of money. It was always: "Bess just bought a new colour T.V.; Bess got a new Persian rug, a new car, a new dishwasher." On and on it went until Berna began to feel inadequate because they couldn't afford these things in the same way Marc's sister did. In any case, her values were quite different. Berna was weary when Marc left to go back to work, and often sighed with relief, though she loved him.

It was now a month since Marc had been at home with Bess. Quite often he lay on the sofa with his eyes closed, though he was not asleep; at times when his grey eyes opened, they took on a glazed look, or else he would close them tightly, as if trying to blot out something. Lately, he had not been eating well and he was losing weight. He smiled as he looked at himself in the mirror, saying, "Berna would be happy to know how slim I'm getting."

Bess came in with a bowl of soup and said, "You have got to eat, Marc. You can't survive this way. What are you worrying about?" She thought he was being stupid. "I drive you around in my new Cadillac, I buy you clothes, and don't you like the new T.V. I got for your room?"

Marc replied, "Oh, yes, Bess, I love it. I like everything we do, but I don't want to talk just now."

Bess felt she was becoming as lonely as she had been before he came. He seemed to be always daydreaming. His excuse for not conversing with her was, "I'm not feeling well." This had been his constant phrase. Placing the soup nearby, she said, "Please do have some of this soup. I made it especially for you." Then she quietly slipped outside to the front porch and sat down to think.

As she rocked in her favourite chair, she tried to think back over the last few years. Marc had always seemed extremely happy when he came home to visit her. True, he didn't always bring his wife, but she had never encouraged him to. She remembered she had told him many times, "Your wife seems not to love you. At least here you know for sure that you are loved." He always seemed to glow when he heard that.

"I love my brother," she told herself fiercely. "I want him beside me. We were born together, we grew up together, and hopefully we will die together, or at least near one another. I won't have anyone coming between us." So saying, she pressed her lips tightly together just as Marc often did when he wanted his own way, and said, "He will be happy here, I know. I will make him happy."

With this thought in mind, she decided to devise ways to cheer him up, though one thought nagged at her. *Surely he's not hankering for his wife and daughter. They are strong and healthy and Berna is quite independent. He is a sick man.* Of this she had convinced herself two years ago when he had a thyroid operation.

Mind you, it was Marc's wife who had nursed him back to health, though he had been restless after a month in bed and wanted to go see Bess. He confessed to Berna at that time, "I miss Bess so much it hurts." Berna never could understand Bess's power over him, because they weren't identical twins, yet Bess dominated him even from a distance.

Unfortunately this domination was a hangover from their teenage days; when their mother was alive she often despaired of them with this attitude. Poor Len had had his fair share of it from Bess, but because he loved her so much and was 20 years her senior, he understood her shortcomings and could cope with her egotistical domineering attitude without offending her too much.

On the other hand, Marc's wife, who was young, found it all very wearying, though for love of him she tolerated it and made brave attempts to steer his attention into productive channels, hoping that eventually he would be rid of it. She soon realized Bess's influence was always a step ahead of her; his twin had such a stranglehold on Marc, who was the weaker of the two emotionally, that he succumbed to her wiles easily over and over. At times, Berna thought, *that Bess, she is an evil person, while Marc is so naïve, he can't see her for what she is.*

Bess even penetrated his thoughts. At times, he and his family would be happily involved in doing things, when suddenly Marc would mention Bess and then his whole attitude would change to one of discontent and dissatisfaction. Berna actually was prepared when he left; she had often wondered when Bess would claim him. Berna said to her girlfriend once, "Marc is so trusting, he never realizes that Bess is subtle, conniving and an emotional thief. He never feels manipulated by his sister; the sun always rises and sets on Bess, and she glories in this adoration, yet I pity her, and at times I pity him."

Bess was always possessive through their youth. She had made Marc be friends with her friends, go to the movies she wanted to see, to parties she preferred—it went on and on. She had managed to break up many a love affair of his with her lies. Of course he didn't dream it was her doing. Now she had taken him from his family, and yet she could not understand why he seemed to be ill and deteriorating. She still put it down to his thyroid condition, which was actually no threat to his well being.

In actual fact, Marc was fretting for his family but hated to talk of it to Bess for fear of her reaction. He was torn between his love for her and his fear of her, yet he loved his family. He said to himself, "It's so unreal. I am just realizing how much I have lived the life Bess wants me to. She has made me do things I haven't even wanted to do, and now I am actually afraid to upset her."

It was unfortunate that Berna had simply accepted his desertion. She had cut herself off from him completely. When he telephoned to tell her he was not returning to her, she had told him. "Marc, I did try my best with you, but now you have chosen your path in life. Little Jenny and I will therefore take ours. You have always been free to visit or go see your sister at any time. I have never criticized her. She has been good to you and I know you love her. After all, she is your twin. God bless you. I hope your happiness with her will be justified." And she hung up. When he tried to get in touch with her some months later, she had left no forwarding address and had no listed phone number.

He wished he could see them now, but he could not even go to look for them. He was totally dependent on Bess for everything: money, clothing, food, and everything else. And he couldn't bring himself to discuss the problem with her. His fear of her seemed to loom darkly over him, so he gradually fretted himself sick, lost weight till he was down to 120 pounds for his 5 feet, 11 inches.

Bess, meanwhile, hovered around him like a mother hen, worrying about him, making delicacies to tempt him to eat, asking friends to come and visit so as to occupy his time and make him talk. Then she brought him things like a diamond ring, a new colour T.V. for his room, a new suit, shirts, a radio. Still he displayed that deadpan expression and glassy look in his eyes, which she hated but could not erase.

When some five weeks had passed and Marc did not improve, she asked her own doctor to come and see him, because by now he refused to go out and would barely eat. He would not talk to her and nothing seemed to interest him; he wouldn't even look at T.V. programs with her. He spent most of his time lying down.

When Dr. Garcia came, Marc was in a state of inertia. He had even stopped taking his thyroid tablets, which were essential, though not life saving.

Dr. Garcia was concerned that Bess had taken so long to call him in. He said to her, "He has lost his will to live. I will have him hospitalized."

Bess sat with her brother night and day at the hospital and tried to get him to talk about what was bothering him, but he refused. All he kept saying was, "You are a good and loving sister, Bess," often with tears in his eyes.

One night about five days later, Bess went outside for a breath of fresh air while Marc seemed to be sleeping. She finally wondered whether she was to blame for her brother's condition. Unfortunately, it was now too late for such thoughts.

Just then the doctor called to her, saying, "Your brother has just slipped peacefully away in his sleep."

Bess was devastated. She ran inside and hung on to his lifeless hand, saying over and over, "My brother, I love you, I love you, I love you. No one else loved you like I did."

She cried non-stop for almost an hour and had to be led away by the nurse.

One thought struck her, and it hurt her deeply. Never once could she remember Marc saying in all their years together, "I love you, my sister." He had merely followed her lead and told her often that she was a good and loving sister. She still did not realize that she had only possessed him and not loved him.

Marc had finally figured that out too late, but the smile on his lifeless face seemed to reveal the happiness he felt in being free at last from his dominant twin.

The Return

Joe stood at the school window pensively watching the huge snowflakes pummel down. With long, slender fingers he stroked his thinning black hair. Through the half-opened door of the hall behind him, he could hear Miss West, his assistant history teacher, remark to Tom Teems, "I hope Johnnie gets here soon. This is foul weather for driving tonight. We need to get home to Reading before it gets worse."

Joe's mind was alerted when he heard the name Reading. *So that's where she lives,* he thought. At once the thought of spending the long weekend alone in his two room kitchenette apartment in Manhattan appeared bleak and depressing. He wondered what it would be like to visit his birthplace after 34 years. His thoughts rambled on, *Funny, I know her well, yet never knew her hometown.*

When Joe was 22 he had graduated from Pennsylvania State University with a Master's Degree in History and even now it pained him to think back to that day. He and his parents had just arrived back in Reading when the accident happened. The car had careened off the road in the dark of night and his mother, a kindergarten teacher, had died instantly. After the funeral and clearing things up, his father, a civil service worker with the Pennsylvania State Department of Commerce, took a special assignment to go to the Middle East while Joe moved to Pittsburgh. There he had taken a teaching post in the History Department for 12 years, and though there was ample opportunity to re-visit Reading, he just couldn't bring himself to do so.

Now he was Head of the History Department in the New York City's Lincoln High School. He had accomplished this childhood dream, but somehow it held no real glamour, for these days he felt so alone and depressed. Without realizing it, he had heaved a big sigh and said aloud, "I just couldn't go back after all these years."

Just then Marion West came out with her suitcase and, overhearing him, asked, "Go back where, Mr. Hicks?"

A bit embarrassed to be thus caught, he replied, "Oh, I was just being reminiscent and wondering what Reading was like now."

Marion put down her case and looked closely at him, seeing an average, thin, rather forlorn-looking bachelor, and her heart warmed to him. She had always had a soft spot for him and liked him. On impulse she said, "How would you like to come home with my brother and me to Reading for this Remembrance Day weekend? You'd get to see Reading as it is now, and I think you'd like my family too."

Joe took off his thick glasses and wiped them carefully before replying. His blue eyes squinted as he tried to see her clearly, "Thank you Marion, but I don't think I'd fit in with you young folks."

"Nonsense," she replied. "I'm not that young. In any case, I know Dad would enjoy your company. You both have lots in common, like hating TV. And like you, his hobby is reading about the Civil War. Oh, he too was an air raid warden in World War II."

Joe's sad looking face brightened at these words and he began, "Well...." Marion cut him off. "Do say yes. Mom loves having another man to fuss over."

Actually Joe had been visualizing such a bleak weekend, for his only friends were his school colleagues and they were all going home or visiting someone for the holidays. He decided then and there, "I will go with you, and I hope you don't regret the invitation. I'll do my best to fit in."

Marion thought, "That's one hurdle crossed. Time enough to get him interested in me as a person later on." To him she replied, "That's the spirit. Johnnie should be here within the hour. We'll stop by your place so you can pick up a few things. Is that okay?"

"Oh, sure, it won't take more than five minutes."

"All set then," said Marion.

Johnnie, Marion's younger brother, soon arrived. He liked Joe on sight and, in the car, spoke jovially with him so that Joe felt he had known him a long time.

Johnnie asked him, "How long have you been teaching? Does Marion pull her weight as your assistant? I hope you don't let her put one over on you."

Joe found himself laughing a lot, something he hadn't done in a long time. He began to feel relaxed.

Joe Hicks had not returned to Reading since that fatal

accident and he had not wanted to, even when his Dad had died in Iran. He did all the legal business regarding the family home by mail and phone. The memories were too acute still, and he had misgivings as to how he would react now. His family had been really very close-knit.

Marion's Mom greeted Joe so warmly on arrival. "Welcome Joe, we're so happy to have you stay with us. I hope you'll enjoy being here for the weekend. Just relax and join in."

Then Mr. James gave him a welcoming hug as he said, "It's good to see you at last. Marion has mentioned you, but just barely."

He replied, "I'm glad I came. I was born and raised here you know."

"Oh, that's wonderful. This town gives one such a warm feeling."

Joe felt compelled to say, "I guess so, but," he continued, "it has painful memories for me. My mother was killed in an auto accident here at a crucial time in my life. My Dad and I both left afterwards and never returned. He's dead now too."

"Dear, dear," said Mrs. James. "I can feel your empathy, but we'll make sure you have a good weekend. It's Remembrance you know, so we'll have to help you remember and then you can place your memories to rest in proper perspective." And she gave him a hug.

Joe was really touched by Marion's family. He began to look at Marion in a new light. Subconsciously he had always admired her, especially her youthful zest for life. She had always been friendly towards him but very formal, he thought. Now she seemed so different away from the school. Her brown eyes lit up when she laughed, and he even noted she had dimples in her round cheeks. "I feel like pushing back those runaway curls on her head," he said to himself. Then blushed at his thoughts.

After Remembrance Day dinner that night, as they sat having coffee, Mrs. James very quietly asked Joe, "Tell us what happened that fateful night, please."

He was so startled, he stammered, "Oh, no, I couldn't."

She touched his shoulder lightly and said, "Oh, yes, you can. It's vital that you talk about it so you can lay the ghost to rest. You and your Dad bottled up all your emotions inside; they have to be let loose."

Joe swallowed and sighed, then started to speak quietly and slowly. He recounted the events before and after the accident and surprised himself that he didn't shed a tear. He felt relieved as he spoke. The family listened intently, especially Marion, who felt deeply for his emotional turmoil and hurt. She leaned over and squeezed his hand softly to show she understood and was compassionate. When he had finished, Mr. James said, "Don't you feel better now?"

"Yes" Joe replied, "I do, and now I don't feel so hurt anymore. I guess I needed to talk about it. I feel like a weight has been lifted from me. Thank you all very much."

Then he turned towards Marion. What he saw was a beautiful, sensuous woman with kissable lips, and the sight shook him. He was tongue-tied and trembling.

Marion's face glowed as she too realized how he was looking at her. "Let's go outside. You need a breath of fresh air after all that I think," she said.

As they walked through the door to the porch, her Mom and Dad looked at one another and Mrs. James said, "He's free of his ghost at last, but I think Marion has snagged an admirer."

Mr. James replied, "The Return to Reading has been the best thing to happen to him all around, I think. We'll just have to wait to see what happens now. I do like him and I think Marion does too."

Together they started clearing the dinner table and told Marion's two brothers to help them and then sent them off to a movie.

Needless to say that weekend was the start of a whole new world that opened up for Marion and Joe. Their discovery of a mutual liking and admiration for one another led them both on many fun-filled weekends at Reading. Joe at last felt life was really worth living, and it wasn't long before he asked Marion to be his wife. The Return, as he often referred to that Remembrance Day weekend, was the best thing to happen to him, and he had no regrets.

Creativity

People are fascinating to watch. Sitting on one side and merely watching them proves that God is most creative. Actually, he has endowed some form of creativity in all living things, whether human or not.

Consider this: a human female specimen. There are many facets to her being; she might be tall, average or short. She may be fat, thin as a rake, or pleasingly average in the most physical aspect. Men might consider her the perfect specimen, and drool over her, or some might consider her disgusting. Then there's her gait: an erect walk, a slouch, or she might have a slinky or pert and jumpy walk.

Now the male specimen is not much different in all these aspects. Consider the fact that no two specimens are really identical, even if they are twins.

All these things are only a miniscule part of what goes into the creation of a human being. No wonder there are people who, being creative in their jobs, consider these aspects in relation to their work. It is doubtful that they always realize that they use humans or even animals as their pattern. For example, cars. These can be sleek, stodgy or even pleasingly attractive. We've all heard of the Mercury, the Tornado, the Cougar, and many others that just go from one destination to another. Then there is the writer, the author, who can transport the human mind from the dark ages of history to the imaginary world of fantasy and romance or even war or science.

Mind you, the creative mind works in many ways, travelling many pathways: for good, for pleasure, for business or for evil. From the beginning of time this has been evident. The Bible is full of creative happenings, good and evil. It seems at times some present day humans swallow the evil part of creativity. Man uses his creativity to stalk, kill, rape and make war on his fellowman, while other humans use their creativity to portray beauty, pleasure, good feelings, truth and peace.

It is truly amazing what can be released from one human being via his creative mind. It's true that some people let their creativity lie dormant; they never use it for either good or evil. These people never leave their mark on immortality.

Actually, these are only tiny facets in the creation of man. The human being has such a vast amount of creativity given to him at birth. He can use it or not; he can use it wisely or foolishly; he can reach heights of personal and financial success with it; or he can use it for evil, but the fact remains, he has it and only has to discover it and use it. If every individual used his or her creativity wisely, the world would truly be a happy, peaceful place to live.

True Love

It was the year 1909 and Mary was sure she was in love. Her brown curls bounced up and down like Mexican jumping beans as she ran home from school. She felt ecstatic and her brown eyes shone like stars in her pretty, round flushed face. She hugged her books to her chest and said to herself, "It's great to be in love, but I have to keep my feelings secret, as I know Mom would never understand. I am so happy, I feel I could burst."

Mary was only 15 and she and her mother Grace had recently moved to the small Central American town of Waha, just outside of Belize. Her mother had immediately registered her in the small public school nearby. This was Mary's first day at school and she had sat next to the most handsome boy she had ever seen in her life. He had even asked her if he could sit and have lunch with her outside. They had a most wonderful conversation.

She told him, "I am sure I will like Waha." What she

didn't realize was that this boy, Carlos, had been smitten with the love bug as soon as he had laid eyes on her. Although he was only a year older, he felt electrified to be with her and knew he would never forget her.

Their school days went by in a whirl; there seemed to be a mutual recognition between them. They liked doing the same things, talking on the same subjects; they even liked being quiet together. They became really good friends and were inseparable.

Unfortunately, Mary's mother had a set plan for Mary. Grace had always worked hard to look after her daughter and herself. No one else mattered to her. Mary's Dad had disappeared when the girl was only three years old and Grace tried hard to forget that incident. She did scrubbing, cleaning, washing, ironing and cooking for many homes from dawn till late at night, and was glad for the money she was paid. She wanted the very best for Mary, her only child. She considered Carlos, Mary's new friend—a penniless boy of sixteen with parents as hard working as herself—did not figure in her dreams for Mary.

She loved her daughter. Mary was a beautiful child, tall for her age. She wrinkled her pert nose when she was happy but her eyes often betrayed her when she was unhappy, at which time they resembled dusky little pools about to flood over. Grace watched her daughter and realized she seemed to be fascinated with Carlos, so she often warned her not to get too cozy because he had no future to offer her, as his family was "as poor as we are."

Mary therefore learned not to let Grace know how much she saw of Carlos and especially how much she loved him. The two kids often discussed their own future together and were oblivious to any other person.

About a year afterwards, an American man emigrated to Waha. Being wealthy, he bought the big house next door to the shack where Mary and Grace lived. Mary and Carlos had discussed the man and she told Carlos, "The American man is loud mouthed, ugly and full of himself. He ogles me and I hate it."

Carlos told her to try and keep out of his way and sight, but she said, "It's not so easy. my Mom just told me she is going to work for him starting next week. Every time I look at him, he reminds me of a bulldog." She didn't mention that his eyes seemed to walk over her and undress her. She didn't want Carlos to get annoyed. Little things like that bothered him.

This American renovated the house he bought, sparing no expense, and when it was finished a couple of months later, Grace said to Mary, "We are moving into the apartment Mr. Toms has provided for us, as I will be his housekeeper. We are so lucky."

Mary said to her mother, "I don't like him at all. He is a show-off and he's so short and fat."

Grace replied, "He has such kind blue eyes and such lovely blond hair, I know he's not handsome but he has money."

Mary kept her thoughts to herself because she knew her mother thought money was everything in life.

What Mary didn't know was that both her mother and the American had plans for her. Mary was due to graduate just after her seventeenth birthday. The two adults often discussed how best to handle things as both knew Mary would have objections, considering she was so young and Mr. Toms was almost 12 years older.

For Mary's birthday, her mother told her she would hold a small party. Mr. Toms financed everything; it was like coming-out party. Mary was happy because she had insisted that Carlos be invited. She and Carlos had begun to talk of getting married when she was eighteen and she could sign for herself and didn't need her mother's consent. They both made a pact never to love anyone else until they died.

Immediately after graduation, the blow came. *It's like a death sentence,* Mary thought. Grace called Mary at bedtime and told her, "You will marry Roy next month now that school is over. I have given my consent to him. It will be the wedding to top all weddings."

Mary was stunned; she was speechless. Finally she stuttered, "I can't marry that man, he's too old. He's 35-years-old and he's too ugly."

"You'll have to, replied Grace, you have no choice. This is no time to think of age and beauty. Roy can give you all the luxurious and comforts of life and you'll have money to burn. This has been my dream for you. It is all settled and I've already signed a contract."

"What, asked Mary, what about my dreams, and Carlos?" She then admitted to her mother, "I love him and I won't marry anyone else."

"Be realistic," said her mother. "Carlos is poor, because he has no job or money."

"Yes, but he loves me and we have our own plans for the future."

"They don't count," said Grace. "Roy will build a smaller house for me next door and he'll give me an allowance so I won't need to work anymore. This is everything I have ever wanted."

"It's your dream, not mine. I want to marry Carlos and no one else."

Grace soothingly said, "You'll get over Carlos in time, my child. What you feel is only puppy love. You're too young to recognize real love. It will grow on you, believe me it will."

Mary said, "No, it won't, not to an old man." She stamped out of the room and cried herself to sleep that night.

The next morning on the way to school, she told Carlos what her mother had said. He was extremely indignant. "She can't do this to us." He suggested that they run away, but after much discussion, both realized it would be futile, as she was not yet eighteen.

Every day Mary cried and her once happy face looked pale and pinched. Carlos also was unhappy and felt useless and frustrated, especially as he couldn't get a good paying job. Roy was elated though. He bought Mary beautiful clothes and an enormous diamond engagement ring. Mary refused to wear any of the gifts and was silent whenever Roy came to talk to her. He was very polite and gentlemanly and never once touched her except to give her the ring.

Her mother was furious and every night she slapped Mary until she broke her spirit and got her to submit to the inevitable.

Mary said to Carlos two days before the wedding, "What can I do? I never knew my father, my mother refuses to talk about him or tell me anything. I don't know if he's alive or dead. I have only you. Don't desert me, please," she wailed. "You know you are my true love."

They comforted one another whenever they met. Carlos even contemplated killing Roy, but Mary said that would separate them even more. They made a pact to keep in touch no matter what.

The wedding day dawned. Mary looked like a beautiful doll, but her eyes filled with tears as she walked up the aisle. With many of their schoolmates Carlos stood outside the church watching. He was very tearful and sad. He swore under his breath that he would rescue Mary as soon as she was eighteen. Soon the ceremony was over and she was Mrs. Roy Toms.

In the church vestry, Roy kissed her, then took her in his arms and hugged her very tenderly. He could feel her cringe, yet it bothered him not. He was a self-made man who always got what he wanted. He had wanted her and bought her like every other possession he had. What he didn't know was that Mary had made up her mind that morning as she dressed, that Roy would marry her but he would never posses her. She knew she could never ever love him. Her heart belonged to Carlos until she died, she told herself.

The honeymoon was brief as Roy had much business to attend to. He found her an obedient, passive wife who did everything he asked her to. She did refuse at first to spend his money, but as time passed, she matured and blossomed. Roy was proud of her, yet he never once let her realize that he was hurt by her aloofness and passiveness. She bore him two sons and a daughter by the time she was twenty-two. She discovered as time went on that Roy was really mean, petty and bad-tempered and a miserable companion. He lavished time, money, jewelry, clothing on her, yet never once was she a willing, loving wife.

All through the years Carlos and Mary never lost sight of each other, though there was never much contact. Her mother saw to that as she kept a rigid watch on Mary, even monitoring her going out alone. Distant sightings and brief conversations were nevertheless enough to keep their burning love alive. Carlos worked at small jobs then eventually joined the Police Force. This paid well and had many benefits. Mary loved him even more; to her he looked extremely distinguished and handsome in his uniform.

Mary's mother became crippled with rheumatism and just about this time, Mary started to show an interest in Roy's work and began to be pleasant to him. He of course was elated and happy at this turn of events. What he didn't know was that this was all a cover up for Mary and Carlos's clandestine meetings. Mary's mother was unable to get out to watch Mary's going and comings.

For almost a year Roy and Mary seemed to be friends and a happy couple. Then another son was born. At a glance it could be seen that the infant was an exact duplicate of Carlos, with curly black hair and eyes and chubby face with a sparkling beautiful smile. He had a lovely Latin complexion like Carlos.

Roy realized he had been taken for a fool. He was absolutely furious and beat Mary black and blue. Her mother had no sympathy, said she deserved it, but Mary told Roy, "Having my son was worth everything. I have no regrets."

Roy ignored the child but Mary lavished all her love on him. After another year, she had a daughter. Roy was doubtful whose she was. In complexion she was like Roy but in her beautiful face, she certainly looked like Carlos, for Roy was no beauty.

Roy realized he was playing a losing game but being an influential wealthy man, he used what tactics he could. He managed to get Carlos transferred to another town. Mary and Carlos were broken-hearted but managed to keep in touch by phone and to see each other sporadically with the help of friends.

It was when Mary was 25 that Roy decided to seek comfort elsewhere. He didn't actually plan it. He had been feeling very lonely and at a party he met a rather homely, though kind woman, who seemed saddened at his unhappiness and frustrations. She was easy to talk to and of course he used his money as his usual bait, but Ursula didn't care about his money. She genuinely liked him for himself. She had been born with a crippled leg and no one had paid her any attention until Roy came along. She was grateful and full of pent-up emotions, which she lavished on him.

Mary noted that Roy began to change and she found he was not acting mean, bossy or demanding. She realized after talking with friends that he had found consolation elsewhere and she decided to seek a divorce. Funnily enough Roy was actually relieved to grant this, though he had always said he never would.

He had come to a point in his life where he realized that Mary would never love him or submit to him. Her heart was only for Carlos and Carlos was her one true love, long before he came on the scene. He finally realized that not everything could be bought with money. He admitted this to Grace, Mary's mother, when they discussed the divorce.

Six months after the divorce became final, Carlos and Mary were quietly married and immediately moved to another town. The children enjoyed having two homes. Roy generously provided for them all, but young Carlos and Mary were Mary's special loves. Eventually Carlos retired from his job, the children grew up, and Grace passed on. Carlos and Mary went to live in Europe. On the day she died, at age 85, her last words were "I've never regretted loving you Carlos. You are the only happy event to happen in my life. You are my one true love."

The Birthday Gift

As she entered the tiny apartment she shared with her long time school friend, Jenny picked up the mail. Immediately she noted the Italian stamp and knew her godmother had remembered her upcoming birthday.

"I guess she has sent the usual cheque," Jenny said to herself, feeling elated at the thought of some extra cash to spend.

Jenny had never met her godmother, who lived in Venice, but knew she had been her mother's dearest friend. They had gone to school together and corresponded frequently when her mother was alive.

Her godmother had never forgotten Jenny's birthday or special occasions, like Christmas or Easter. Being very well off financially, she always sent a generous cheque for which Jenny was extremely grateful. Her spirits always

144

brightened when she read her godmother's letters.

Jenny's aunt, who brought her up after her mother's death, had recently died, but her godmother did not know that there was no money forthcoming. Jenny did not inform her of that fact.

She flopped her slender body down on the well-worn sofa, pushed back a stray brown curl from her forehead and proceeded to open the letter. Her brown eyes widened as she read, and she kept repeating, "It just can't be true. It just can't be true."

Just then her girlfriend arrived. Seeing her sitting in an obvious dazed condition, Carol asked, "What on earth is the matter, Jenny? You look shocked and flushed. Are you alright?'

"I think I'm numb," she replied, handing over the letter. "Read this Carol, then tell me if I'm dreaming."

Carol sat down next to her and as she read, kept saying, "Oh, my goodness". Suddenly she leaned over and hugged Jenny, saying, "It *is* true and I'm so happy for you. You WILL go of course? Knowing how shy Jenny was, Carol feared she might be hesitant and refuse.

Jenny's godmother, Elaine Sutherland, had written in her usual formal manner, wishing Jenny a very happy twenty-first birthday, She had enclosed a return ticket for Puerto Rico, a paid booking for two weeks at the Hotel Condado, plus a most generous cheque to cover clothes for the trip and spending money. An extra cheque was enclosed with a note. *Get your friend Carol a pretty dress too and both of you must go out to a nice restaurant and celebrate before you leave for Puerto Rico,* it said.

As the girls re-read the letter and discussed the exciting news, they noticed the postscript. It stated, "My husband's nephew, Darin, works in the Hotel Condado and will be expecting you. I know you'll like him. He's tall, good-looking, kind and hard working."

"Your godmother is always so generous, and though I have never met her, I think she's a bit of a romantic. Darin is probably a young eligible catch," Carol told Jenny.

"Oh, dear," said Jenny, "he's most likely as formal as his godmother".

Wrinkling her pert nose, she continued, "But I'll keep an open mind and try not to get involved." They both smiled at this.

"It would be a perfect ending," said Carol," if he was young and fell in love with you. Knowing how reserved Jenny was, Carol hoped there might be some excitement for her.

Jenny smiled. "Actually, I wish Godmother hadn't added that bit about Darin. He's probably a playboy and you know I mistrust those types. Nevertheless, I will be pleasant to him and will tell you all about it when I return."

A week later Jenny arrived at the San Juan Airport, smartly clad in a salmon pink suit, looking very chic. She heard herself being paged. As she approached the airline counter, a tall, well-dressed, handsome, sun-tanned young man with green eyes and tousled, sandy-coloured hair materialized at her side.

"Are you Miss Hoy?" he asked, gazing into Jenny's eyes.

"Yes, I am," she replied, thinking he was from the airline.

"You are just as Aunt Elaine described," he smilingly said, as his eyes took in her slim, well-curved figure, manicured hands, and even her tiny, well-heeled feet. He was smitten speechless.

Taking her hand, he said, "I'm Darin. I am so happy to meet you." He spoke with such ease and friendliness that Jenny forgot her shyness. She felt confident that she would enjoy her vacation if he were as nice and comfortable to be with as he seemed.

On the way to the hotel, he took care to point out sights. Upon arriving, he told her he had ordered a tray of food to be sent to her room, as by now it was past midnight. They agreed to meet for breakfast.

The first week, he took Jenny everywhere when he was not busy.

I'm really having marvelous time, and seeing a lot of the island, she wrote on her card to Carol. The fact that she knew she was losing her heart to him, she kept to herself. She was a bit disappointed that the feeling appeared not to be mutual but she consoled herself with the thought, *maybe he'll say something before I leave.*

Two days later, the bomb fell...or so it seemed to Jenny. They had just returned from swimming, when he was greeted most affectionately by a rather vivacious blonde dressed in a stunning blue outfit that matched her eyes perfectly: eyes which seemed to say, *Hands off Darin.*

She acted very possessive and quite sure of herself. Jenny's shyness returned in full force and she withdrew into herself. She felt she was no match for this girl.

Darin greeted this creature like a lost kitten, yet more like a sister. After the necessary introductions, he invited Vana (that was her name) to come along on the next day's outing. Jenny sensed that this idea did not please Vana, but

Jenny decided to go along and see what would transpire.

The next morning, as they walked around old San Juan, Darin was explaining to Jenny about La Fortaleza, the President's palace. It was then Vana became impatient.

"Darin," she whined, "you know how I hate this part of the city. It's so boring. Surely Jenny can find someone else to take her around. Let's do something exciting."

Jenny noticed Darin's flush of annoyance, but before he could reply, she said, "Vana I understand. In any case there are tours from the hotel. Darin has enough to do in his job without having to bother about me."

Just then a bus stopped at the parada (bus stop) nearby, and before either could reply, Jenny boarded it. Just then she heard Vana laughingly say as she put her hand in his. "You, a job?? That's a joke, isn't it?"

Darin waved frantically and called to Jenny, ignoring Vana.

Thankfully the bus was prompt and roared out of sight. Jenny was trembling with emotion and tried not to cry. Darin was obviously in love with Vana. That was probably why he never said anything to her. All these thoughts swirled in Jenny's head.

She wondered, though, why Vana seemed to think Darin didn't have a job. Her godmother definitely stated that he worked at the hotel. On reaching her room, Jenny felt it was time to take stock of her feelings. She didn't want to be involved in a triangle. She really liked him, even loved him, she admitted to herself, but didn't want to hurt him. She decided there and then that it was time to return home. She had enjoyed her time in Puerto Rico, but she didn't want to get hurt either.

At suppertime, he sought her out as usual and invited

her to go dancing. Though her heart ached to go, she feigned tiredness and pleasantly refused, hoping she had hidden her feelings for him well.

He appeared hurt at her refusal but accepted it, saying, "Then I'll see you at breakfast tomorrow. Have a pleasant night and sleep well,"

After breakfast the next day, he went into the office to do some work. Vana came in just then and sauntered over to where Jenny sat. Very sweetly she apologized for her attitude the day before.

"Darin's position as co-owner of this hotel with my Dad is a delicate one where guests are concerned," she said. "I know he's been overly nice to you, but that is just to please his aunt. He'll forget you once your trip is ended. Then we can go ahead with our marriage plans."

Jenny was flabbergasted at Vana's revelation and tried hard to keep calm. She was hurt and disappointed, but she had good composure and was now glad she had decided to leave.

"I understand the position," she told Vana. "Darin does not interest me, so there's no need for you to worry." She then excused herself and went to her room.

As she packed and dressed, she couldn't help thinking how Darin had misrepresented his position to her. And to think, she thought he might even be in love with her. She fought back tears and was glad when she managed to leave the hotel without seeing him.

As her taxi halted at her airport terminal and Jenny got out, there stood Darin. He didn't say a word. He paid the driver, took her arm and luggage. "Where do you think you are going, Jenny?" He asked, "without even saying goodbye to me?"

Though stunned to see him, she said, "I am going home where I belong. It's time my vacation ended. I only came to please my godmother after all. I have had a nice time, thanks to you, and I have enjoyed myself, but I have had enough."

"Well, I haven't, young lady, and I think it is time we had a talk."

"Why talk to me? Talk to her, after all you are going to marry her. Go away and leave me alone. I am going home." She started to walk away.

"Marry Vana? Are you nuts?" Darin said, laughing. "She is a spoiled brat with an over-active imagination. I am *not* in love with her. I'm in love with *you*."

Jenny stood still as he continued. "I spoke with Aunt Elaine last night and told her I was in love with you. I promised her I would wait until today, your twenty-first birthday, before I spoke my mind to you. I told her I would ask you to marry me and she gave me her blessing."

Jenny's heart soared. Explanations could wait. She couldn't believe her ears. Darin loved her. This was the best birthday gift ever. Darin hugged and kissed her. "Do you love me Jenny?" he asked anxiously. "Please say you do."

"Yes, indeed I do," she replied as she hugged him, "but I was afraid you didn't love me, that you loved Vana."

"Vana was never in the picture, " Darin said. "I humour her for her Dad's sake. He owns the hotel. I really and truly only work there."

He then told her, "Aunt Elaine is going to be very happy. She's dying to meet you, you know. I think she planned the whole thing."

I wonder," mused Jenny. "She always seems so formal in her letters, yet warm and inspiring."

Darin called a taxi on the way back to the hotel; they were making plans to visit Aunt Elaine. "We'll finish the rest of your holiday by making plans for our wedding," Darin said.

Jenny was so happy, she felt she could burst. She was dying to tell her friend Carol about the wonderful turn of events.

Jenny thought this was the best birthday gift ever. "Now, let's have the talk," she told him, linking her arm in his on entering the hotel.

Tabbie

It was in 1988 that my daughter, Anita, brought a tiny black kitten no bigger than a mouse home from school in her backpack, and we had to feed her with an eye-dropper for quite some time but she thrived. She was a Burmese that Anita had rescued from drowning by her owner in a garbage can next to the school. Four others had already drowned.

After a few hisses and attempted scratches, she bonded well with our old male cat "Ginger". She grew steadily—having a glossy black coat—was very energetic, playful, and loved to explore. Eventually we had to keep her on a leash in the backyard, and even then the birds were in jeopardy.

She was upset when Ginger passed on at age 20. Tabbie kept good health, and was a good companion. She made us aware that she owned us, not the other way around. She was loved by everyone but always maintained a special attachment to Anita, as if she was grateful for being rescued.

At age 15, she suddenly stopped eating. We were worried and took her to the vet. He ran numerous tests, x-rays, etc. and even put her on a drip for dehydration. She kept getting weaker and eventually we had to do the inevitable.

It was so sad to say goodbye, but she seemed content and ready. We hope she's happy wherever she has gone. We will always cherish our fond memories of her for all time. She is sadly missed by her family.

Afterword

This is written for my family so that they may know what my life was like—the people and events that shaped it. I hope it may be of interest to them and perhaps offer some help in their lives.

I found life interesting, was a thoughtful person, quiet and reserved. I enjoyed everything I did because I wanted to do it. Mind you, when I was young, there were things I was compelled to do because I was a child. My regret is that I did not then have the ideas, time and opportunities to do some of the things I now know about. My life would have been so different. My advice is to have dreams and be positive and work towards implementing them. Let no one deter you from accomplishing them. Without dreams, life is not worth living. Now read on.

I was born in Belize (then known as British Honduras) at almost midnight on 28 February 1924; I just missed being a leap year baby. My appearance was loud, to say

Afterword

the least. My parents were Marie Lopez Fuller and John E. Fuller. Health-wise my mother was in bad shape at my birth, so I spent most of my first months with my maternal grandmother, Anita M. Lopez. She loved me and cherished me. My bonding was with her and when I could make discernible sounds, I called her "mama". That lasted till the day she died.

At age one and a half, the family immigrated to New York City to join my aunt and uncle, but when I was around four-and-a-half years old, my father decided to return home. It was a bit sad to leave my older cousin, Bill Kittiel, and my aunt Daisy and uncle, Alan Lopez. These are my mother's siblings.

I was a very outgoing child and was doted on by my father until the birth of my brother six years later. I was literally told to "get lost" (because I was just a girl). It became worse as I grew up, because my father constantly told me that girls were stupid. My grandmother helped me through this stage.

In college, I didn't talk much but was a brilliant student. I was even labeled "Miss Perfect" and considered a snob. The kids enjoyed picking on me. Fortunately I had a champion older friend, Ioane, who saved me many a day by beating off my tormentors.

At age 10, unfortunately, I was ill with a leaking heart, whereby I was not allowed to participate in sports or dancing. This was traumatic for me, believe me. Also many kids did not understand the situation. They thought I was just being more snobbish. Actually I was extremely shy. I could not even walk fast or ride my bike, and missed out on so many activities during that three-year period of my life.

Canada

I immigrated to Canada in 1961. I think after travelling to Mexico, Puerto Rico, Guatemala, Spanish Honduras, Jamaica, Nicaragua, my homeland had become boring and I wanted to expand my horizons. I had planned to stay 15 years, save enough money to return and set up my own business. This never materialized, as I got married and then with all the bad changes in Belize—crime, drugs etc.—I didn't really want to go.

In Canada I worked first with the YMCA of Canada Head Office, and it was during that time (1961) that there was a Hurricane "Hattie" that hit Belize badly. I volunteered to work with the Canadian Red Cross in the disaster. I was given the usual medical shots, a uniform and instructions, and was sent by Royal Canadian Air Force plane along with a male Red Cross Disaster worker. I ended up in Belize working for four months. It was the most enjoyable job I ever had. I was well paid but I would have done it for just meals and lodging.

After the YMCA, I worked at Toronto General Hospital as a Medical Secretary, a new career for me. Later on I worked with the University of Toronto: all very interesting and exciting. It was a learning experience. My last job was at the Hospital for Sick Children as Executive Secretary to their Chief Pathologist, Dr. M. J. Phillips, who was also a Liver Research Scientist. I retired from this job at age 65. After six months I worked part-time with a popular lawyer, Charles Roach. I enjoyed this, I guess because it was about law that I liked, another learning experience.

Reflections

ACCOMPLISHMENTS

It might seem that I did not accomplish much, because I am not rich or popular or acquainted with the cream of society. Nevertheless, I personally feel I accomplished a lot. I did finish school at the top of my class, I won a Scholarship in Social Work and attended the University of Puerto Rico for eight months and graduated. In 1958 I was given a Silver Medal by the Queen of England for my volunteer work with the Girl Guides of British Honduras. In Canada I attended the University of Toronto for two years. I worked hard all my life. In Belize, along with my regular day job, volunteer work with YMCA and Girl Guides, I raised chickens and ducks, made hams and bacon and marmalade for sale. I also taught piano lessons and had quite a few graduates who passed their exams at the Academy of Music in London, England.

Reflections

TRAVEL
I travelled twice to England and to Europe, visiting Belgium, France, Holland, West Germany and Luxemburg. I enjoyed those trips. I also travelled all over Central America and Panama and Mexico. I travelled through the United States a lot with my husband. He worked as a seaman on the Great Lakes and died in 1985.

FRIENDS
I made some lasting friends in school, Girl Guides and YMCA. We are still in touch, though some have passed on. I also enjoyed and had pen pals from schooldays and have met four of them personally: one in California and three in England.

There were the usual boyfriends; we went to movies, parties, dances and picnics, but none seemed to hold my interest. I found most of them irresponsible, having no positive dreams or ambitions and wanting two and three girlfriends at one time. I detested the ones my father chose for me. His idea was for me to marry a man who could support me and buy me a good home. I wanted someone to love me first and for us to work together to accomplish our dreams.

I got married at age 42 to Fred L. Carroll, a fellow Belizean who had immigrated to Panama at 19. We met by chance. We adopted one daughter, Anita, at age six months. She is a North American Chippewa Indian from the Huron area of Canada.

SCHOOL

I started at Gibbs Private School on returning from New York. I loved school and my teacher. Learning was a breeze for me, lots of fun and games. I learned to read and enjoy it even to this day. My favourites were comic strips and still are, although I am in my eighties. At school, we were taught social graces; I had piano lessons, learned to ride a bike, etc. I was given everything for that era, as apparently was customary.

At age 9, I was transferred to St. Hilda's College, an all girls' school. We wore white uniforms, and had classes from 8 a.m. to 1 p.m. Teachers were mostly from England and it was run on very English lines.

Learning was easy for me and I was always at the top of my class. I even took extra classes offered: bookkeeping, typewriting and shorthand, with no problems. I loved school, although being extremely shy, I had problems socially. All I really wanted was to make friends but I had a fear of rejection. At age 15 I passed my Senior London Cambridge Certificate and my Matriculation Certificate from the University of London, England. I was really ready for the working world, but unfortunately too young for it.

I therefore started as a student teacher at $5.00 per week, teaching kindergarten in 1939. I took classes after school and earned my Teacher's First Class Education Certificate in 1940. Mind you, life was no bed of roses, due to my shyness. I had not received much demonstrative love from my parents, though I knew they did love me. My father was a chauvinist and thought females were only good as housewives. My mother was a weak nervous type. My ambition became to definitely NOT be like either of my parents. My grandmother was very loving, helpful person and guided me in my ambition. I wanted to be myself, different, not one of a crowd; even in clothing I made up my own styles and created my own hairdos.

I must say here my grandmother was a very independent and positive person. She could have written the book of Positive Thinking. She didn't have much schooling but was a self-taught person and had strong beliefs and faith in God, which she passed on to me. She was no coward and had definite standards and a moral code she lived by.

THE GIRL GUIDES/GIRL SCOUTS

I had been a Girl Guide since age 11, and at age 16 was elected with another Guide to represent British Honduras at an International Conference in Massachusetts, U.S.A. This was thrilling for me and most exciting. It was my first taste of independence because the other candidate, Jerry Craig, (a year my junior) travelled with me first by a small boat to Puerto Barrios, Guatemala, from the Port of Belize and then we were transferred to a huge tourist ship there and travelled to New York City. It was an unforgettable experience for both of us. Seeing the Statue of Liberty at sunrise in New York harbour was an awesome sight. In Manhattan we were entertained by very rich society ladies who were on the Board of Directors of the Girl Scouts of America. It was a treat for us to visit these posh homes. At the Camp (Camp Bonnie Brae) in East Otis, Berkshire Hills, we met and talked with girls from many countries around the world, but the highlight of the trip was when Lady Eleanor Roosevelt and the President visited. He stayed an hour (no photos allowed), but Mrs. Roosevelt stayed all day and I actually had my picture taken with her and another delegate. I often recall this trip with fondness.

When I left my teaching job at St. Hilda's College, I took a job with Government as Security Secretary at the Defense War Office during World War II. I worked with people from Scotland Yard and M15 from England. After the war, this office was merged with the Police Department (still as Security). I then became the Private and Confidential Secretary to the Commissioner of Police. I held this position until I retired after 15 years, due to medical reasons.

I did enjoy working at the Police Department and it was exciting being involved in murders, crime, drugs, etc. firsthand. Plus I was the only female working there. Left to make my own decision, I would not have worked as a secretary. I wanted to be a lawyer or Social Worker but my father held the purse strings (and scholarships were not yet heard of), and he wanted me to be a pharmacist, which I hated. In those days, women were supposed to work temporarily, find good husband and settle down to a home and children.

VOLUNTEER WORK
During the 15 years I worked with the Police, I was also a Guide Captain of a troop of 15 girls. Later on, I became the Commissioner of the Girl Guides of the British Honduras. I really enjoyed my time spent there.

I also joined the Young Women's Christian Association

when it started and was their first secretary. In both associations, I enjoyed every minute, doing what I liked best: helping people. I ran my own Girl Guide Camp and did two camps for underprivileged children for the YMCA. The Police Department gave me time off for this.

In 1958 I went to Puerto Rico on a U.S. Social Work Scholarship to the University of Puerto Rico, where I graduated with a Certificate of Achievement in Social Work. This was an exciting time for me, as I met people from all around the world and learned many things about life in general. I loved Puerto Rico and I had no difficulty in understanding their language because Belize also speaks Spanish.

PHILOSOPHY

My philosophy of life has been to do good whenever and wherever I can, and to have faith in God. I feel one gets out of life what one puts in, be it good or evil. I try never to hate anyone, try to be forgiving and tithe my earnings. This practice has repaid me a hundredfold.

I try to believe the rule: "there is always a bit of good in everyone", and I never sit in judgment on anyone. Over the years I learned not to trust strangers. I feel I pass a place once and should do whatever I can to assist as the occasion arises. One thought I would like to leave to my family is "whatever you do or dream you can do, begin to do it". You have genius and power if you trust god to be your partner; we are all His children.

Use yours talents to the fullest and never let anyone tell you you can't accomplish something. Rich is not necessarily cash; we can be rich in good friends, love and affection of family. Loving yourself is also important; always be optimistic. I hope I have been able to be of some help and comfort to someone I passed on my life's journey. I feel I did my best for my country, my family and friends. Their appreciation is immaterial.

'

Anna Carroll
Autobiography

Anna Carroll was born and educated in Belize (formerly British Honduras) in Central America. She loved writing from the time she was in school. She is a retired widow and lives most of the year in Florida with her daughter. The rest she spends with her brother and his wife in Canada.

Her pastimes are reading, writing, crochet and doing puzzles, She also loves to cook.

82205415R00099

Made in the USA
Lexington, KY
27 February 2018